ALL SMILES UNTIL I RETURN

ARON BEAUREGARD

Copyright © 2021 Aron Beauregard

All rights reserved.

ISBN: 9798764969411

Cover & Interior Art by Anton Rosovsky

Cover wrap design by Don Noble

About the Author Art by Katherine Burns

Edited by Patrick C. Harrison III

Special Thanks to Mort Stone for Additional Revisions

Printed in the USA

Maggot Press
Coventry, Rhode Island

WARNING:
This book contains scenes and subject matter that are disgusting and disturbing, easily offended people are not the intended audience

JOIN MY MAGGOT MAILING LIST NOW FOR EXCLUSIVE OFFERS AND UPDATES BY EMAILING
AronBeauregardHorror@gmail.com

WWW.EVILEXAMINED.COM

FOR MY WIFE

It's hard to tell what the meaning of all this is, but existing makes sense because of you.

"Unlike life, when books become meaningless, they are making a point."

- Mason Cooley

A NORMAL DAY

It was a day just like any other; ordinary in the most painful way. It was like watching paint dry on a cold sore that was never going to heal. It was bullshit. It was minutia. It was life. I suppose it had gone on for far too long anyway.

To the people that sat around me in the endless rows of dingy cubicles, I was just another underachieving dude chained to a computer and telephone. A well-behaved bird chirping out exactly what I'd been told to. Regurgitating the emotionless script of the commercial gods from corporate prison, a deadness living in my gut like I was with stillborn child.

On the outside everybody looked at me like a ray of sunshine; someone that put on the smile daily like Mr. Rodgers. That's what they wanted, right? Leave it all at the door and pretend it doesn't exist. If you told yourself everything was okay enough times, you almost started to believe it.

The truth was it was all a façade. One grand, masterful illusion for the ages. I saw the fractures in the forced grins as well. Maybe we were all aware but just too pulverized to discuss it. It wasn't as if a conversation would change anything. It would just lead to more of the same. Evolved manipulation tactics, new framing, a Candy Land-worthy sugar coating that would rot your sweet tooth and send a diabetic tits-up in an instant.

That was the game. Those at the top of the food chain said we were doing the right thing. We needn't question it; it was simply the way things were. That was what working for Bank USA was all about; following orders.

The policy was as clear as crabs; eat shit, let that shit you ate simmer for a few, then throw it up into the ears of whatever poor bastard was calling. It should be so nutty and thick that it clogs their canals. Snuff out the communication by leveraging policy designed to target the downtrodden.

I have no idea how I was able to do it for so long. The maddening mumble of white noise. The delirious drone of the dial tone. The grim glow of the monitor. The murderous threats of the customers.

I had a particularly good one that morning. I mean, some of these conversations you just can't make up. Some of it was just argument for the sake of argument.

"I didn't write the check!" the man with the Nigerian accent yelled.

"But, Mr. Nnadi, you agree that Jason Reynolds is in fact your landlord?" I asked.

"Yes, but I did not write a check from my savings account! It is fraud!"

"Sir, this is a money market savings, which has check-writing capability. I've already reviewed your checking account, and as I stated previously, no check cleared for your rent there like every other month. Is it possible that you just might have grabbed the wrong checkbook?"

"NO! IT IS FRAUD! TRANSFER ME TO THE FRAUD PEOPLE!" he screamed, his extreme pitch causing my headset to crackle.

"Let me just lay this out once more, just so I have it straight… You're saying that someone has stolen your money market check book… and committed a fraudulent transaction by… paying your rent? Your rent, which, in addition, you've consequently overlooked for the first time since you've had your account with us…"

"YES! TRANSFER ME!"

He wasn't wavering from his nonsensical stance. The conversation had reached a level of dumbness that I was no longer willing to participate in.

"No," I replied. Technically, we weren't ever supposed to deny a client from filing a claim, but I just couldn't entertain the man's lies any longer.

"WHAT?! You don't tell me no! What—What is your name? I want your full name!"

"Okay, my name is Andy Cameron. That's A-N… D-Y—"

"Hold on!"

I waited for him to finish his snail-pace note-taking and give me the okay to continue.

"Okay," he prodded.

"And my last name, Cameron, is C-A-M… E-R… O-N," I replied nonchalantly. Just as the last letters left my jaws, I saw my manager, Tatiana Mornar, rise up from her cube and signal to the team.

"Log off!" Tatiana yelled to everyone.

The weekly brainwash meetings were all we had to look forward to in the office. It was better than talking to the madness that was on the other end of my line.

"Okay, Andy, let me speak with your manager," the customer replied.

There was no fucking way I was going to prolong this pointless call; lies were in order. He'd served up a little more shit than I was willing to swallow.

"I'm afraid she's unavailable at the moment. But I can have her call you back shortly. What is the best number to reach you?"

"I WANT TO SPEAK WITH HER NOW!" he screamed, achieving the pinnacle of irate.

"Once again, she's unavailable now, so we can end the call, or you can give me your phone number for follow up. What'll it be?"

He finally submitted and rattled off his phone number. I asked him to slow down in a semi-rude fashion like he'd done to me. Except I wasn't taking any notes; that asshole wasn't getting a call back for his ludicrous inquiry. Not on my watch. It was a truly childish tactic, still, it made me feel just an eyelash better about the daunting exchange.

To hell with him, I thought, setting down my headset and locking my machine.

I normally didn't raise that tone with customers. I usually had more empathy, even for the idiots. But lately, it had become more of a pattern. I'm not sure exactly what was responsible for the shift in my character, but it felt good not to take shit from them. Unnecessary shit was the worst kind, and it was all that seemed to get hurled at me.

I walked down the long stretch of hallway and followed Tatiana and the rest of my teammates. Suddenly, a profound sense of dread took over me; they were headed to the calibration room!

To a relatively quiet, keep your head down and work guy like me, it might as well have been a Nazi torture chamber. There was little else I loathed more than hearing the sound of my shrill voice and having my shortcomings dissected in front of a group of my peers.

In many ways, group calibrations were like sitting down and having a nice slow game of Russian roulette. Going in, we had no idea whose call was getting picked or how many bullets would be in the chamber so to speak. We also had no idea what kind of a mood they were gonna catch us in on those recordings.

Were they going to get us on the day we were running late? On the day we had a screaming hangover? On the day we decided to focus on what absolute fucking lemmings we'd become? It all depended on what day Tatiana pulled the call from. It all depended on the luck of the draw.

Immediately my brain scrambled backward searching to remember the last time I'd had a tiff. My heart was racing, my palms were sweating. I couldn't think.

Eventually I accepted it; when I walked into that room whatever was going to happen, was going to happen. But little did I know, the call review set to transpire would be the least of my problems.

THE HIDDEN CRITIC

Tatiana meant well, but she wasn't doing anyone any favors. That included both her associates and the customers. She was drinking the Kool-Aid mixed with Jim Jones' semen. Pridefully a servant to Bank USA, she swallowed the gunky and hypnotic concoction with a wide-eyed adoration, begging for more at the conclusion. The toxic structure had risen into her mind, congealing upon her tired brain, turning her into a modern-day meat puppet.

As a Croatian immigrant she grew up with little else than the beautiful facial structure that God had granted her, and a pair of tits that I stared at with a deep fondness every time I had morning wood that lingered into the office. Her accent was comical at times; she often mispronounced words, but not in a way that made them so you couldn't understand. It was typically cuter than anything, I suppose.

But when the words started to cut and scrutinize, that foreign charm melted away. When our numbers were coming up short and her superiors required justification, that poor girl from a third-world village came out gritting her teeth.

"This month's metrics are deplorable. The way this is going, I'm not going to have a job much longer," Tatiana confessed, looking down at the colored sheet that was mostly red and yellow with just a peppering of green cells sprinkled about.

"The surveys have never been worse… JC wants answers so we are going to have a double-calibration today. We have to find out what's been bothering our customers so much. The time should allow us to listen to at least two calls from everyone."

Me and my ten other peers were crushed to learn it was a back-to-back session. The color drained from our faces as we looked back and forth at each other like a bunch of confused cattle. It felt like we were about to take a beating from a disappointed parent.

No one was more fidgety in the entire group than Phillip Marks. The collection of pens attached to his pocket protector clamored together emitting a faint metallic scramble. Phillip pushed his thick obtuse glasses from the tip of his nose back toward his squinting eyes and the wet cowlick haircut that sat above them.

Phillip couldn't sit still, which wasn't entirely abnormal, but it seemed a bit much, even for him. His sweater was unbuttoned, but it still seemed too hot in the room for his attire. The sweat streaked down from the nerdy crown of his head running off his baby face. I thought I had trouble getting laid but this fucking guy was hopeless.

He raised one of his chewed-to-the-cuticle fingernails and asked, "Tatiana, may I please get my water bottle?"

She looked at him a bit perturbed. It seemed like an excuse to escape the room for a few minutes, but what could she say?

"Quickly, Phillip," she huffed, knowing she'd need to wait another moment before starting now.

The greasy goober disappeared through the metal door and the rest of the team anxiously chatted under their breath. I watched Tatiana as she began to initialize the projector and key-up the audio.

I angled my chair sideways so it pointed toward the screen. While some of the other team members chatted quietly amongst themselves, I glanced over at the beautiful woman who'd interestingly chosen the seat right beside me.

Janie Watson was a sweet girl, someone who always seemed warm and approachable (even though I never had the balls or reason to do so really). I felt my nerves flare whenever I was in close proximity to her. My palms got sweaty and I couldn't seem to verbalize basic sentences anymore. Something about her completely captivated me.

I thought it was silly. She was married with a pair of young children. Why did I need to be nervous? Why around her? There were other girls just as striking, just as sweet, that I felt completely at ease with. But not Janie.

I didn't want to try and explore the reason for the feelings she spawned inside me. It was pointless to do so. I wouldn't.

Should only be a few more minutes until my doom, I thought, switching my focus to Tatiana's cursor that hovered over my name on the screen. A thirteen-minute call from the thirteenth of March is what was on display for the entire room.

What day was the thirteenth? My mind continued swirling with anxiety and trepidation as I glanced at the calendar on the wall. *Fuck! That was a Friday! Friday the 13th!*

Fridays were never a good day to pick, and Tatiana damn well knew it. At the end of the work week associates on call were just staring at the clock. Waiting for it to turn. Waiting to run free from their headset shackles, throw back a half-dozen drinks and forget about what their lives had become. If there was any day that we were more likely to give some snooty lackluster service, it was then.

Not only is it a Friday, it's fucking Friday the 13th! When all the wackos and loonies are out. The selection couldn't be more—

My thoughts were cut short by the muffled disturbance pushing its way through the metal door. "Phil! What the fuck are you—"

BANG! BANG!

Tatiana's eyes widened and I quickly turned around in my seat. What was all the ruckus about? As I peeled my sights off the projector screen, I realized that the call displayed on it was no longer relevant. There was a far bigger fish to fry now, one that had been swimming in a sea of depression and silent rage for far too long.

When I got my head around, the door was already closing. Phillip Marks locked it, and the echoing sound of screams leaked in from a blend of genders in the hallway. The pistols in each of Phillip's hands were shaking with fury. The man was at his wits' end.

Most of the people in the room began to shriek or gasp instantly, but I was more stunned than anything. A crippling paralysis took hold of me and I did the only thing that seemed logical: I prayed.

God save me, I will do anything, ANYTHING YOU WANT!

It sounded so fucking silly and pathetic looking back on it. As if a voice was just suddenly going to appear and say, "Well, if you promise to donate more to the homeless and not jerk off so much, I can fix this for you."

In that moment I realized most people never seem to acknowledge God until they need him. Until their reality or current situation has gone so far down the fucking toilet that there is no way in hell to get out of it. Then we start talking crazy. That fella in the sky we weren't sure we believed in, well, he's as real as rain in that moment.

I wondered if I should have tried to connect with the higher power previously, building up some clout for a situation like the one I was facing.

After unsurprisingly getting no answer, I watched Janie

Watson, the sweetest twenty-four-year-old mother of two I'd ever laid eyes on, begin to panic. She stood up and started begging like a panhandler during rush hour.

"I—I have a nine-month-old and a—"

The shot left the barrel before I could learn the age of my coworker's other child. She must've told me or the team before. I was probably too busy staring into her lovely, heartwarming hazel eyes to store it in my cerebral hard drive. But now it seemed more important than I ever could have imagined, as I considered those might be the last words to sprout from her lips.

I watched the bullet rip into the side of Janie's petite neck, her blood splashing all over. She fell back into my lap. Her comforting eyes transitioned to orbs of dread as she grasped at the wound on her neck and began choking violently. It was crystal clear to me that God wasn't prepared to answer my prayers, nor anyone else's. We were on our own with Phillip.

"Keep her down there," he commanded, staring at me coldly.

We'd never had the best relationship, but it was pleasant. The old uncomfortable nod, bogus smile, and occasional awkward sentence summed up our interactions. I hoped more than anything that he remembered that I'd never been a dick to him.

"Everybody stay in your seats!" Phillip sounded so timid even when he was yelling and holding a gun, but his gusto couldn't be questioned, not with poor Janie bleeding out in my lap.

Her hand had fallen off her neck as she squirmed around near my legs.

"Try to relax, it's gonna be okay," I lied.

Blood both launched and oozed rapidly from the small hole torn in her throat. I clamped my hand firmly around her neck like the Boston Strangler, doing everything in my power to keep as much of the red inside her as she started to pass out.

"No! No more calibrations, no more anything, you understand me!" Phillip screamed at Tatiana.

"Yes, Phillip, it's over. I won't play anything," Tatiana confirmed.

"This is the last place I ever thought I'd end up, pulled by your strings in any direction you and those fucking corporate pigs see fit. Forcing me to explain a $35 overdraft fee for a cup of coffee to a woman with a hungry, crying baby in the background! It's madness! No more! It ends today. No more goddamnit!"

"I—I can get your customer's overdraft fee refunded, I promise you. Any fee you need I can have it overridden. Just put the gun down, please," Tatiana begged.

"That's like changing one lightbulb in Vegas, no one would even notice. But if you switch electric companies…"

Phillip was mumbling madness and I could feel more of Janie's blood squirting out between my fingers with each word he spoke. *What is he planning on doing?* I wondered. Whatever his warped plan might be, I hoped it would be executed quickly. It didn't seem like it was going to take long for Janie to bleed out.

"Whatever you need, just tell me, Phillip," Tatiana said as calmly as her shaking tone would allow.

"I'm afraid your humanity has just hit a wall, Tatiana. Y*ou're* overdrawn, and your karma account needs to be rectified immediately," Phillip explained, raising the pair of Glocks level with her beige blazer.

Some people in the room shrieked, most covering their eyes. I would have liked to but I had to hold Janie's neck together. So instead, I watched.

As the shots entered her body she gyrated unnaturally. The holes in her chest looked small, not what you'd expect from watching movies. But the streams of hot blood shooting out and the disturbing wheezing noises seeping out of her Swiss cheese lungs made up for the missing horror.

"Help me," Tatiana pleaded.

Her words were easily overshadowed by a nasty gurgling noise. Tatiana squirmed around in her chair in wide-eyed anguish. Clearly disoriented, she grabbed at the air beside her. Seconds later she toppled over, falling on her side as the faintest trace of vitality left her vessel.

Nearly the entire rest of the team was crying and begging. For some reason all I could think about was Janie. I didn't even have a spare moment in my racing mind to consider keeping myself out of harm's way.

"Everyone fucking relax!" Phillip screeched.

There was still plenty of sobbing, but for the most part, everyone was pretty quiet after he made this request.

"I'm not here to hurt you. It wasn't any of you that caused this to happen. You're all just like me; you had no choice. I just killed Jake Cardel before I came in here. Guess they'll need to find a new site lead now. But I didn't kill anyone else. JC fucking deserved it; he was the face of this corruption. Actually, it goes much further up in the hierarchy, but this is about as high as a fucking peon like me can reach. And—And you all are very familiar with Tatiana already. She never fought for us. She never fought for the people we rape with regularity. She only dug us in deeper. She acted like she would die for this pathetic leech of an institution… and die she did," Phillip explained slumping down into Janie's empty seat.

I stared into his maddened glare. He sat inches away and all I could do was try and swallow the lump of fear in my throat and keep my hand around Janie's leaking neck.

"So don't worry, I'm not going to kill any of you, just myself."

Phillip said he wasn't here to hurt us, but then why was Janie's gory, hot throat still sitting in my hands? I gazed into her fading wet eyes; she still looked beautiful somehow, even after being made a mess of. She was the kind of girl I wish I had the balls to ask out or strike up a conversation with. But people as sweet as her were always taken, and rightfully so.

"What about Janie? She's fucking bleeding out, man. We need to get her to a doctor, fast," I piped up.

"I'm afraid that's not possible, no one leaves this room until I kill myself," Phillip replied.

"Well?"

"Well, what?"

"I just told you, she's dying man, can you just get it over with so maybe she still has a chance?"

I never imagined I'd be trying to expedite a suicide. On its face it sounds crass, but within the bloody context of that day, it was more than proper.

"I can't just do it right away… I need to think first, okay? And frankly, all your talking isn't helping. You're really starting to fucking piss me off, Andy."

I don't know what came over me. Maybe it was less about emotion and more about status. I had nothing.

No family.

No real friends.

No pets.

No purpose.

What did I have to lose exactly? Another twenty-thousand days of smarting redundancy? Listening to that dreadful alarm tear up my eardrums every morning, the nausea setting in? Picking up a phone eight hours a day and getting cussed out? Heating up my Ramen mid-day and my Hungry Man at night? Watching the Giants go six and ten every year?

After my spontaneous and discouraging self-assessment, I remember the thought in my head ringing loud: *Please, fucking take me, I dare you…*

I couldn't convince myself to care about the imminent danger surrounding me, but I *could* convince myself of one thing: Janie was an awesome girl.

She had some young children back at home and a real purpose. Anytime our paths had crossed, she'd seemed genuine. She didn't deserve to fade away in some shitty call center. This was just supposed to be a stepping stone for someone like her. I wasn't about to give up on her because Phillip needed time to think.

I snatched her off the crimson carpet and stood up. My movement stunned Phillip, he shot up from his seat to point both barrels at my face. I took my hand off of Janie's neck and cradled her with one arm and then used my free hand to reach for the twist lock.

"SIT THE FUCK DOWN! NOW, ANDY!" Phillip yelled.

The blood continued to spurt from Janie's wound, painting my chin and collar, as I turned back to Phillip.

"I'm taking Janie to the emergency room. You do what you've gotta do, Phillip," I replied, unlocking the door in front of me.

My fingers slid down to the metallic handle and I began to turn it, but I would never get that door open. Unbeknownst to me a different door was about to be exposed. One filled with a foul darkness and nightmarish makings that I never could've imagined.

THE DARK VOYAGE

The tunnel was filled with utter nothingness. People say they see a light at the end of it; people say they see their family and friends. People say it's a feeling of pure elation, like they don't want to leave. The stories couldn't be further from the truth.

It felt like a roller coaster, a venomous vibe lingering in my belly as I sped faster and faster into the black. Normally a scenario such as this would have had my heart jumping out of my chest, but there was no activity. I still had my emotion but I'd been robbed of the carnal feeling I'd come to know; the ticking of my body's clockwork had ceased.

I wasn't even truly sure that I could see anymore. Maybe if my other bodily functions had shut down, so had my vision? I had no way to be sure, I just had to wait for whatever was going to happen, to happen.

It felt like I'd jumped out of a plane, with gravity a thousand times stronger than I'd known it to be. It was hard to understand time anymore. Whatever was happening felt like an eternity. I could've been there for days but maybe it was months or weeks?

I also couldn't hear anything. Considering the speed I was moving, it felt like there should have been wind flapping against my frame and whooshing all around. It was just an incredibly heavy and uncomfortable silence.

But the smell…

The smell was there and like nothing I could come close to branding with a proper description. The raunchy wave could have only been a combination of things from my experiences but even that didn't do it justice. Something like if mold, maggots, rotten flesh, and fermented pus had all hung out in reality show fashion, stewing in a filthy grease trap for months. It made me want to puke but my vessel was no longer abiding by the rule set it used to.

I found myself thinking about my folks. It was weird because I never knew them. Every time I thought about them, I had to put a face to it. So, they always appeared how I imagined they might look. My dad was a bit like me but older, and my mom was quite different but had a very kind expression soaked into her skin.

They just left me on the steps of a particularly cold and transactional establishment for castaways and never looked back. I had no one except for the carousel of boys shuffling in and out before I could learn how to socially interact with them. Some people get picked last in dodgeball, but I got picked last in life.

Growing up as an orphan was bad enough, but never getting placed was the absolute shits. At least if you had foster parents you could sort of pretend and put a face to them. Embrace the façade and be proud. Other people didn't have to know and you could blossom into whatever you aspired to be. But my memories always felt pathetic; a total fabrication of what life was supposed to be like.

As pitiful as they were, I could still picture my thoughts. At least I still had that much. But suddenly the silly renditions of my parents disappeared. Not because I'd stopped thinking about them, but because there was something before me now I hadn't seen since I reached for that door handle: color.

But it wasn't the color I'd hoped for. It was red. The best I could figure was that I was dead. There was no other explanation for my heart stopping and everything I was witnessing. I was dead and headed towards red.

I could only base what it was supposed to be like on the stories and television shows I'd heard people relaying their experiences on. I had no other reference or curiosity on the topic. People that died and got brought back to life on those shows all seemed to say the same thing; white light, family, friends. But what I was seeing looked like a pit of carnal crimson, and it was only getting closer.

All of the sudden my hearing returned. The clanging of chain was the first noise that I heard. As I descended from the darkness at free-fall speed, my drop stopped abruptly when I plunged head-first into the redness.

I hadn't noticed initially due to the rapid impact, but the lake of death was actually bubbling. The searing thick stew danced violently, and as I entered it, the scalding lumpy moat invaded my orifices in full force. The wicked soup caused my skin to blister and erupt, I could feel the meat slipping off my fingers, the bones uncovering, my eyeballs melting.

My vision had been robbed, but the agony remained. I couldn't tell if it was psychological or physical pain that was tearing me apart. It was probably both, but it was becoming difficult to tell the difference.

Whatever it was it birthed the worst feeling to ever befall me. Torturous, tedious, yet somehow not terminal. I wished that it was, but I had a strange epiphany in that instance: when you're alive, a lot of times you wish you were dead. You never really expect it to be worse though.

My body was on fire, a million needles and knives felt like they were going in and out. I was begging in my brain. I don't know who I was begging to, but I begged.

PLEASE STOP! I CAN'T TAKE IT ANYMORE! I pleaded.

Just like back in the calibration room, I wasn't expecting an answer, and I didn't in that instance either. But I was taken aback when a booming but languidly calm voice in my consciousness replied, "Oh you can, and you will."

THE AWAKENING

Sometime after the voice had spoken to me, I lost the ability to move. I never lost consciousness but it was just a whole lot of nothing; the waiting room between worlds I presumed. My senses had been stripped as bare as my body. I was just a blank, crumpled canvas, a manifestation of the macabre, awaiting whatever came next.

My surroundings came back into focus slowly. At first my vision was only a dull shade of murky whiteness, my hearing was a faint metallic ringing, and what I smelled was just a tinge vomitous.

Gradually I regained my motion. My fingers were still a bit boney, and as I pressed them against each other I could feel the slimy muscle and tender meat beginning to swell over them. I didn't realize it initially, but I could feel my flesh beginning to regenerate.

I understood that the dingy white that was obstructing my vision was soft sclera establishing itself, and as the pupil formed the curtain was lifted. I was hung upside down, thick chain surrounding my raw ankles, and where those chains led there was no way to know.

The sinister black oblivion that painted the skyline of nothingness above me struck a sense of fear inside me the likes of which I'd never known to exist. When I followed the chains further above, they eventually disappeared into the permanent midnight, but far away there was something there. Something dark. Something wicked.

The road to revelation led me to gaze upon a wet set of orbs that watched me. The blood bags were overfilled to the point of hyperextension, but still their limits remained intact. The freakish fluid inside caused the exterior lining to mutate and contract. The soup of sin in each of the bowls festered with what appeared to be schools of unusual organisms and plump parasites.

They stirred in frenzy and seemed to be enraged by my presence. Their tiny teeth, strange antennae, sharp whipping tails, and tangled tentacles made the piercing peepers abominable. While I turned side to side in discomfort, I studied the area around them for any other normal semblances of a face. The darkness below manipulated my mind; I thought I saw a mouth but couldn't be sure it wasn't a figment of my imagination on overdrive.

Why am I squirming? What happens if I fall? I thought. I'd been so distracted by ominous orbs above me that I hadn't given myself a moment to consider where I was even trying to escape to.

I twisted my scabby neck around and looked toward where I thought the ground would naturally be. The area was illuminated in magical fashion; there was light, yet no identifiable light source. That wasn't the weirdest thing I was dealing with, so I quickly moved on from the notion and focused on what I could see.

The boiling crimson pond that I'd been dunked into still

remained, but now I could see the edges of the shoreline. The material looked squishy, slick, and rosy. It reminded me of the gum tissue that housed my own teeth, just on a more massive scale. Not only did it serve as the shoreline but also as walls. There were several gaping cavernous holes that led into obscurity; tunnels of unknown…

Then suddenly, those gloomy tunnels became entrances for evil. Hands and feet and tongues and legs and arms and necks and eyes and hair. It was all there and so much more. The dozens of unspeakable globs of monstrosity that pulled themselves through were like nothing I'd ever seen or imagined.

Arachnid in their general architecture but everything else was human; it was just all in the wrong place or duplicated to the point of delusion. A dozen or so bloody legs and arms acted as stilts for the first one. On its top sat a massive mouth that stretched the length of its body, which was about the size of a full-grown bull.

Several neck-like extremities stretched up toward me, and at the end of each of the elongated flesh tubes were two pincher-like nails. The brittle dead cells scratched against each other like sharp fingers down a chalkboard. I could hear them cracking and breaking with angst.

It felt like I was elevated high enough to be on the roof of a house. The space should have been enough to separate us, but it wasn't. The veiny volume of the deformed limbs increased exponentially. There was no escape from that thing or the countless others that surrounded it.

I looked back up at the fat red eyes. The blubbery transparent casing was shaking even more violently as the gnarly creatures inside sloshed around. And underneath them it appeared. What I thought I'd seen in the darkness was in fact there.

The pointy dagger-like teeth grinned, exposing a vile joy on the being that watched me from above. Its mouth drooled down and the sudsy saliva splashed into the crimson pit beneath me. Upon entry, the girthy dollops of fluid created a splash-back from the scalding ocean that narrowly avoided my tender casing.

My hypnotic disgust from the overseer was interrupted by the sting on my back. Several pairs of the razor nail pinchers had inched their way up to me. My flesh was still sore when they tore into it. The tissue around my bones had just reset and my entire exterior had just begun to scab over when they started in on me again.

The first one wrapped around me from behind and each of the nails stabbed through my cheeks. They pulled down aggressively, snapping my mandible off sideways and slicing into the edges of my neck.

Another one yanked one of my legs free from the chains and folded my calf forward. The other end of the pincher applied steady force to the back of my thigh. Once it had the proper angle in place it crushed down with the pressure of a garbage truck, caving in my knee in the opposite direction. The joint popped and the ligaments and tendons tore and twisted. A cornucopia of gore, bone, muscle, and other mixtures were bound together on the back of my knee like a human sushi roll.

I was really becoming familiar with pain on a level to which my body, had it been properly operational, would have surely knocked me the fuck out long ago. Instead, the agony persisted. Quite a bit of me had been deactivated, but all the receptors that instilled fear, horror, and hideous discomfort remained functional. The design was evil; it was the blueprint of a thousand paper-cuts.

The pinchers picked me apart like a worm between a pack of feisty fouls. Skin ripped, organs were extracted, and the blood bled generously. I tried to scream with no jaw but little came of it. They hadn't taken my eyes yet, so I just decided to close them.

I needed a distraction from the bloody blanket party. I still had my thoughts and remembered who I was. Unfortunately, that was part of the problem. I didn't really have a whole lot to escape to.

I could think about the parents I didn't have or the movies I used to watch. But nothing would be enough to distract me as I felt the sword-like dead cells stab into my rectal tissue.

Janie… Janie was a good chick… hope she's alright…

It was pretty sad. All I could come up with to think about was a girl that didn't even know I existed. A girl I didn't want to admit I had a crush on. A sweet person with the softest, most loving stare. Someone that didn't deserve a bullet in the neck.

As the refined, moist fingernail continued to penetrate me vigorously, I tried to exhale, quickly recalling that I didn't actually breathe anymore. I pictured her smiling face within the darkness created by my eyelids. It was the best distraction I could conjure.

I hope you're having a better go of it than me.

BURSTING WITH DEATH

When my mutilation was all said and done, the heathens had spared my eyes and the upper area of my skull. All that remained of my tattered body was bones and bits of muscle. Somehow my lone skeletal leg was still locked in the chains I dangled from. My ensnared status continued.

As the nerve endings regrew and the muscle manifested upon my claret-caked bones, I rekindled my trepidatious romance with agony. The intimate entrapment seemed to be all I had for as far back as I could remember. Time was always a funny thing, but when every conscious second is occupied by primal pain tolerance, the never-ending nights seem a lot longer. Everything was eternity.

The deformed demons had dissipated, but the wicked enflamed orbs above continued to study me. Once the rough scabs had reformed, I wondered what was next.

I looked back down at the ocean of putrid plasma that still puckered with fury beneath me and then back to the mysterious tunnel from which the evil entities had been bestowed upon me. It might have had something to do with the relentless tortures that were being perpetrated against my body, but my instincts told me that was where I needed to go.

Once my jaw structure was restored, I decided to unhinge it and have a word with the thing in the black sky. "Why are you doing this?"

Its moon-sized eyes didn't blink and its razor-blade mouth didn't move, yet the words still wormed their way into my skull.

"I'm preparing you," it replied.

"Preparing me? Preparing me for what?"

"Eternity."

The heavy word echoed about in my head, slamming over and over repeatedly like a jackhammer.

"Is this… is this Hel—"

"SILENCE!"

The shrill screech of the being left my brain feeling like it'd been shredded with a table saw.

"You must explore me, and I must explore you."

A greasy, ebony tongue slithered out from the being's mouth and pulled the chain I dangled from over to the flesh-scape beside the scalding pit. I laid motionless on my back, awaiting the thing's direction.

The charcoal tongue returned to its mouth but not before ripping the chain off my foot. The ferocity of the removal skinned it from the ankle to the toes and left a glossy, wet sheen coating it.

It exploded with laughter that only grew louder and louder. The cryptic cackle sounded like war. The screams, slices, explosions, gunshots, and mechanical doom was splitting my eardrums. The pitch caused the thing's massive red eyes to shudder uncontrollably. Then, without warning, they ripped open.

The floodgates let loose and the strange raspberry syrup splattered all over my sore body. It was like being hit by a mini tidal wave, but it wasn't the fluid that concerned me so much as what I had seen swimming inside of it.

The outlandish elements contained within the fearsome cornucopia of subspecies that had been stewing and studying me, invaded my body in many ways. If they didn't land near one of my holes then they made a new one. Slowly but surely the bumpy tails, chattering teeth, moist tentacles, and other evils carved their way inside me.

I felt them dallying around and taking control of every fiber of my being. At first it seemed more experimental, the things piloting me around, feeling out the range of movement that could be achieved. Before long, they took a look back into the darkness shrouding most of the red pit, and then turned to the tunnels. I guess I wasn't meant to choose my own route, but the things inside me propelled me to the left-hand path.

My walk was anything but normal; I was moving like a baby deer that had just found its legs. I supposed it didn't matter; embarrassment was no longer a thing.

The meaty subway pulsated and throbbed but remained close to my body. The drizzly blushing walls contracted like aroused genitalia, making way for me with each step. The end of the membrane underpass was wrinkled and raw, with a tiny white hole at the finish.

The parasites pushed me and forced my head through the spongy walls. They jostled my body back and forth until I had finally wormed my way through to the other side.

***

Everything felt so fucking authentic. The smell of the claustrophobic cab in the back of the semi stunk of unbathed trucker and tobacco. The litter of porno magazines, empty coffee cups and cigarette boxes made it seem like home to a lonely man.

I was still naked and covered in mushy scabs that hadn't quite solidified. When the things brought me to my feet, I was in a squatting position, trying to keep balance while the vehicle moved along at a high speed.

Before I could fully register what was going on I was in the front seat of the cab reaching for the handle. The bearded hick in the driver's seat was surprised when I pushed him out of the opening door and took his place. His body hit the hot tar below, accompanied by a sickening thud.

I took hold of the oversized steering wheel with one hand and the clutch with the other. In my possessed state I had no choice but to pop it into top gear. I was along for the ride and rapidly approaching a hundred miles per hour.

What the fuck?! What is this?! I wondered in angst.

When I finally focused on what was on the other side of the windshield, I couldn't have been more horrified.

The police barricade that blocked off the busy country road was seconds away. I blew through the fragile wooden signage as the previously docile officers scrambled out of the way. The sound of shattering wood and crushing plastic filled my ears.

A slew of numbered marathon runners and a massive crowd of onlookers cheering them on were beginning to notice the renegade truck coming full speed in their direction. I imagined that it seemed surreal to them, like it just couldn't be possible.

I reluctantly made them believers as, at the behest of the evil organisms, I began a roadkill run for the ages. The race had become about much more than bragging rights. The unforgiving grill of the truck exploded the first woman I connected with. The fat, dual tires hopped up and down as her body was sucked underneath.

The weight of the mammoth machinery continued over the hordes of competitors, their faces transitioning from a mundane focus on athletic prowess to pure panic and split-second survival instincts. They did everything to clear the way, but for many of them it was already too late.

The spiraling rubber inhaled runner after runner. I felt each of the gruesome bunny hops of the truck's frame shake through my soul. The bumps were brief; the soft structure of their fragile human bodies bowed quickly to the vehicle's destructive density. I could feel their limbs mashing, their torsos crunching, and their skulls exploding.

After what felt like hundreds of additional death-dealing connections that undoubtedly left a long, red trail behind me, my hands jerked the wheel to the shoulder of the road where the crowd was lined up like a school of fish in a barrel.

Screams and carnal destruction echoed into the skies as I continued creating a pulpy path of pure carnage. The ghoulish soundtrack of my terroristic rampage haunted me.

The *popping* of heads.

The *snapping* of skeletons.

The *mashing* of meat and muscle.

No one was safe. My speed slowed slightly as the broken bodies tangled in the tires and underbelly of the rig. I pulled the truck back onto the road as another patch of terrified runners tried to pull away from the impending doom as it rapidly approached them.

The speed of the pursuit and eager evil urges that were fueling it caused the vehicle to tailspin. The back box of the truck twisted sideways until the entire thing turned. The morbid momentum jerked my cab awkwardly and moments later I flipped sideways into a ditch.

It didn't take long for a mass of enraged survivors to smash their way through the already broken windshield and pull me from the vehicle.

The group proceeded to batter me sadistically, my face, legs, and torso absorbing their wrath. Anywhere they could stomp or punch, they did. As the pain once again resurfaced, their bodies started to change. While they stood over me, thrashing wildly, their arms became soupy and began to transition from typical looking skin into a pink slush.

As animalistic screams exited their airways, their runny

bodies melded to the open surroundings, until I found myself encompassed in a giant ball of liquified flesh. The darkness resurfaced, and as the collection of tormented souls faded, the walls of the glistening tunnel that I had just pushed myself out from returned.

In front of me sat another ghastly puckering hole. The parasites, navigating my body quickly, put me back on my feet. They angled my gaze into the strange pulsating gateway once again, then sent me diving right through it.

***

The walls I was enclosed within were mostly white with a very light green highlighting some areas of the newborn nursery. A handful of babies laid innocently in their comfy little beds, their entire lives ahead of them, while a pair of perplexed parents looked on through the protective glass.

They more than likely weren't expecting a naked and bleeding human scab to be dallying around such a sensitive area. The confusion quickly morphed into pandemonium when I zeroed in on the tender soul they were beaming their love at, taking the baby by the neck and lifting it from the bassinet.

The mushy feeling of tender tissue in my hands made my heart ache. *What am I about to do now?* I wondered.

The mother stared on with horror as the father ran to the door; it was locked. I palmed the child's head in my hand firmly; it was no larger than a grapefruit and felt similarly soft. I looked at her with apologetic eyes, but my actions were in stark contrast to my feelings.

The baby's skull went face-first and smashed into the glass. It let out a horrifying crunch and agonizing muffled squeal. The facial fractures and rapid blood loss were the ultimate nightmare for the child's folks. As I pulled the caved-in front of the face back, I wished I could stop it. In my mind I begged the things, but they had no interest in listening.

The second thrust was even more disheartening as the newly developed aspects of the young one only further flattened into a pancake of perversion. The blood splattered outward in various directions like an abstract painting.

The mortified mother's eyes bulged. While she cried the father ran down the hall looking for help. When I peeled the pulpy dome off the drenched glass, I noticed a small crack had formed. I looked at the quaking hunks of head and bone that twitched in my palm before cocking the destroyed newborn back once more.

This time the baby's skull exploded, sending an eruption of brain, blood, and bone in all directions. As the glass continued to crack, so did the strained woman's psyche. The spiderweb of transparent barrier began to crumble and the scream of the broken guardian ripped through the shower of sharpness.

I held the baby's headless frame and rocked it back and forth as if I was trying to help put it to sleep. The frothing mother came through the newly established opening with both arms outstretched and dissolving.

By the time she reached me she'd morphed into a pile of goop that slathered over my body and blocked out all light. It was like I'd closed my eyes for a few minutes as the blob blanketed my body. But before long the wilted watermelon wave of rage seeped into the ground around me and I once again found myself in a tunnel.

I lifted my head up. It seemed even the parasites inside me were beginning to feel worn-out. Nonetheless they aimed my vision toward yet another small opening at the weathered tip of the outlandish underpass.

***

I felt a strange wetness between my legs, pooling around my anus. *What the fuck? What the fuck is going on?!* I didn't even want to imagine what was there, and thankfully, I didn't have to. There was an even more damaging distraction just a few feet away.

The arrangement of flowers that surrounded me looked beautiful, but never would I have imagined the pair of mental renditions I used as placeholders for my parents to be standing over me. Never did I imagine that I would meet them. Never did I believe it was possible for them to manifest.

How is this possible? You're just a thought… How can a thought in my brain become a projection? I wondered.

The people that I always fantasized about knowing but didn't. The people that hadn't done a thing for me my entire existence had finally shown themselves. Somehow the pair of delirious daydreams looked upon me with runny red eyes. In an unequivocally bizarre circumstance, they had waited until I died to finally meet me. Regardless, there they were, standing over my body in the casket, acting sad.

The idea that I'd constructed in my mind of who my parents were and how they should look grieved exhaustedly. The emotions they displayed somehow tugged at my static heart strings, despite knowing that it was all a façade. Still, unsurprisingly, they also enflamed my temper.

I leapt up out of the coffin and grabbed my 'father' by the head and smashed it into the hard wooden lip of the death box. When he fell to the ground, I raised the heel of my foot and drove it into his forehead.

With each stomp my 'mother' cried out. Each thud of my body connecting with his gave me a rush. He was never there for me, only in my mind and at my own expense and creativity. I lifted the tall golden candle stand at my side and drove the circular steel base into his head. Bumps and lacerations quickly filled his expression as I went manic.

"ANDREW!" my mother yelled.

I ignored her and continued to pound on his face, relentlessly tossing in a stiff kick to mix it up.

"ANDREW, STOP IT!" she commanded.

"It isn't me! I can't! I can't stop it!" I shrieked.

Her hyper horrified tone suddenly became calm and

wicked. "Have you tried?" she asked.

Unexpectedly, I slowed my pace. The bloody candle holder ceased its violent actions and I realized that I was in control. I touched the moisture mount still oozing from my anus and peered into the casket.

The malformed lump of humanity, teeth, flesh and tentacles galore, was all heaped together into a sickening sphere of parasitic grossness. The lone eye affixed to the puke-worthy pile stretched a patch of skin over the top and bottom of the orb as if to wink at me.

"You wanted to do it, didn't you, Andrew?" my mother asked. "You wanted to hurt me, and kill your father?"

The bastards had tricked me. They'd released me into the wild amid their mad murder simulation. Into a personal situation that, whether I wanted to admit it or not, I was emotionally invested in.

"What is this?! What the fuck is all this?!" I bellowed.

Blood began to dribble down from my mother's nose. She wiped it away with her sleeve but it wasn't stopping.

"This is you, Andrew!" she howled inhumanly.

"Noooooo!" a voice screamed out from the audience behind us.

I hadn't really had much time to gather my surroundings, but as I used my free will to turn around, I noticed that most of the people assembled were people from my past.

Boys from the orphanage that I'd interacted with for a cup of coffee, teachers, and even employees from the Bank USA call center. But they didn't look how I remembered them. They didn't look well at all.

They were all deformed; noses missing, skin rotten, bug-infested. The smell of decay overpowered my senses just as I was able to focus on the area where the screaming was generating from.

In the back of the death brigade stood Phillip Marks. He was pointing each of his handguns square at the heads of Tatiana and Janie.

"Please don't! Help!" Janie yelled.

"There is no help anymore," Phillip cackled.

I raced down the aisle, flanked by my putrefied peers, and toward the three of them. Once I got close enough, I launched myself into Phillip and we bulldozed into Janie and Tatiana. As our bodies connected, the fluid feeling came back. The bloody bubblegum concoction that had sucked me out so many times already, began to blend the four of us together.

The darkness found its way back to me.

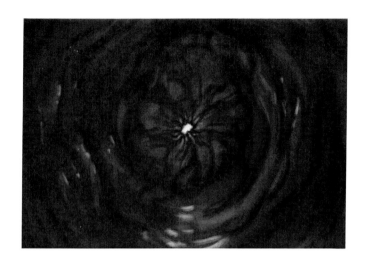

A MORBID MEETING

As the slop that had become us separated, it once again mutated into the wicked walls of our infernal confinement. I say 'us' because, for the first time since the beginning of my dark descent, I wasn't alone.

Janie Watson, Tatiana Mornar, and that madman Phillip Marks all laid equally disheveled around me. Our frame of mind and bodily state was one. Like me they all looked utterly exhausted and traumatized, and like my body, their flesh was desecrated with gaping rips, crusty scabs, and the violence of darkness that had drawn us in.

The nakedness was bizarre; it was something that we all would've immediately commented on in any other scenario except in the impossible one we'd found ourselves in. On any other day we'd have all been breathing heavily, had our routine functions not vanished.

I expected to hear screams roar. I expected to see tears drip. I expected emotion. I saw nothing. It seemed like they were all just lying around, hoping to be left alone. Had they been through everything that I had? Did they encounter the same demonic abyss that had ravaged me?

"Well?" I finally mustered.

"What?" Phillip replied, almost annoyed by the query.

"What the fuck is going on?"

"Excellent question, I'd say we're dead…"

"Dead because you fucking killed us, you bastard!" Tatiana barked, lunging at Phillip and striking him in the head. The blows she delivered were tired and lackluster. It seemed more about displaying the principle of her rage.

"Would you stop it! I've been ripped apart every way you can imagine already. It always ends the same," Phillip whined.

Tatiana eventually toppled off of him and slumped back down on the ground. She returned to her silence and dejection, stewing in our daunting circumstances.

The confusion was beginning to set in. I focused on Phillip and Tatiana for a moment. I wasn't just keying in on their appearance alone, but mostly who they were as people.

"This doesn't make any sense," I mumbled.

Janie lifted her head up and moved the hair hanging over her face sideways. "What do you mean?" she asked.

"If we're dead… if this is it… we certainly went south. I can see why *he's* here," I explained, pointing at Phillip. "And I can't say I'm shocked that she's here," I said, moving my index finger to Tatiana. "But what about us? I'm not trying to sound all high and mighty, but I'm pretty sure I don't deserve *this*. And I'd be willing to bet that you don't either."

"Oh fuck-off, prince charming. Acting like you never screwed up before. Why else would you be here?" Phillip sneered.

"Screwed up! You call mass murder a fucking screw up?! Because of you I'll never see my children again! You're evil! EVIL!!" Janie raged, finding her emotion.

I couldn't blame her for losing it. I figured of the four of us, she was likely the most impacted. She was gutted, no doubt thinking about the little ones she'd left behind upon departing the world of the living.

"Well, if you just would've listened and let me kill myself, it would've only been Tatiana and JC down here with me. I only asked to have a few minutes to kill myself in peace."

"JC? Where the hell is he? Why did we come through individually, but now we're here together?" I wondered.

"Maybe he survived?" Janie interjected.

"Maybe… Let me ask you a question," I said looking Janie in the eyes.

"Okay."

"Do you believe in God?"

"I'm not so sure anymore."

"I don't mean right now. I mean before whatever this is. Did you pray? Go to church? Anything like that?"

"I prayed, I prayed for a lot of things." There was a hurt stewing in her eyes that felt like it was from before she died.

"Damn."

"What is it?"

"I'm just comparing," I said. "I'm trying to figure out what we did to deserve this. In my situation, I never believed. I felt left behind. I *had* no one, I *was* no one. I still consider myself a pretty decent person though. I can't imagine what I did to be handed this. My life was so blank and pointless. It was boring. There was nothing to it, really. So, I was just thinking… I was thinking that maybe it's something I *didn't* do that got me here. But that doesn't seem to be the case."

"You always seemed interesting to me," Janie said. "You did a damn good job seeming busy whenever I tried to talk to you or ask a question."

A smile crept up on my scabby lips. I let my eyes run over her rough reforming skin. Her outline was still one for the ages, and her eyes were incredibly honest and blissful. In a place so warped she took me away; she rescued my imagination and resurrected my passion.

"I was just shy is all. I had a strange upbringing, never quite learned how to interact socially. I guess all that doesn't really matter anymore. We're all just hanging out, naked… so, I feel a little bit more comfortable now. But I'm sorry, I just never really knew how to interact with people. Even people that I would've really wanted to interact with. Like you."

"Well, isn't that just the prettiest little story I ever heard. Reality check! How about you two stop talking about how you got here, or why you got here, and we figure out what the fuck we're gonna do next," Phillip suggested smarmily.

"We? Who said that I'm standing by your side, Phillip? You're a piece of human garbage. A pathetic pissant that only grew a pair when the odds weren't fair. When you had the advantage of a loaded gun in your hand."

"If you'd have just listened, you'd still be alive!"

"You shot me in the back, fucking coward."

"That bitch was already half dead! A third of her damn neck was missing! No hospital was going to save her!" Phillip argued, pointing at Janie. "That was *your* choice, that's on *you*!"

I watched from the corner of my eye as Janie soaked in our exchange. What began as a scowl of anger toward Phillip had contorted and twisted her kind face back to an expression that she was worthy of. It would've felt too self-serving in my mind to tell her I died for her, but I was glad it came out. I was glad she knew the truth. Her flattered smile somehow made me feel strangely better about our grim situation. It was probably because I would have died all over again just to see it once more.

"I may have had to deal with your shit in life, but we're dead now. It's over. Whatever path you choose, I'll be going in the other direction," I explained to Phillip.

"We'll… be going in the other direction," Janie added.

Tatiana had been quiet. She looked like she didn't know what to do or say next. It was as if she was stuck in her own mind and didn't want to journey forward with any of us.

"Wait," Phillip suddenly interjected, almost redacting his forthcoming words before he decided to continue. "I'm— I'm sorry. Things weren't exactly easy for me back then either."

My sentiment hadn't shifted, but as much as Phillip's words and general presence bothered me, I was willing to hear what he had to say.

"It started when I was young, six-years-old maybe. She would come into my room while I was sleeping. I'd be in the middle of an innocent dream, the kind of things that kids tend to dream about. Arcades, candy, then suddenly I couldn't breathe. I would wake up choking, with her hands around my neck or a mouthful of pillow…"

Had he had the bodily fluids to formulate them, the contortion of Phillip's face would have most certainly sprouted tears. There was a lot of hurt inside him.

Phillip dropped his face into his hands.

"She always blamed me. In her mind I was the reason he left. So, Mom said I had to take his place. Over time she explained to me that I had to… I had to make up for the aspects of their marriage that I'd robbed her of. I think I was eight when we started sleeping in the same bed."

Phillip started to tremble uncontrollably.

I looked over at Janie to gauge how she was receiving his confession. She seemed somewhat disturbed.

"She made me… she made me do everything that a husband would normally do for his wife. Everything. I never got to be with a woman I wanted. I was alone. Even leading right up until the end, I was still a slave to her."

I couldn't help but feel pity for him. I'd thought *I'd* had a rough go, but his story was making me reconsider. Maybe being abandoned was a blessing in some ways. It was most certainly better than being entangled in the incestuous relationship that Phillip had found himself in.

"That still doesn't excuse your actions. The hurt that you housed never should have been taken out on innocent people," Janie interjected.

"I know, but my… my brain just didn't work right after that, and I'm sorry. If I could change things now, I would. If I could take it back, I would. All I ask is that you give me a chance. I don't know why we've been put in the same place, but it seems like it's for a reason. I don't want to be alone anymore."

"As horrible as Phillip is," Tatiana said, "I think we need to stay together if we're going to figure out what this is. But there's a good chance, considering what we've been through that it might not even matter. If we're damned, we're damned."

I thought about the concept for a moment and looked back at Janie. Speaking with her directly I said, "Well, I'm not sure how each of you arrived here, but I've been torn to bits and the focal point of unspeakable violence. But my flesh and bones won't separate. It takes time, but I'm always whole again. I don't think we can die because we're already dead."

"It sounds like we've all entered this place under a similar premise. I don't want to rehash all the gory details; I want to try and forget them. However, I would have to agree. But just remember, if there's anything I've learned during this descent, it's that there are things that exist that are far worse than death," Janie explained.

It was an excellent point. I wasn't sure if our strength in numbers meant anything. Nonetheless I nodded my head, allowing Janie to understand that her opinion wasn't being taken with a grain of salt.

Janie let her eyes dart back and forth from the members of our party and found the motivation to stand up. She looked down at us with concern trapped in her eyes. I could tell the pain and anguish of the way things were was beginning to surface inside her again, even before she spoke.

"It's not about me anymore; the only thing I'm focused on is Bell and Alicia. They need me. Their daddy, he… he's not right. Just the thought of my babies being alone with him frightens me more than anything here ever could."

Janie started to pace along the edges of the fleshy pink tunnel in worry. I could see the emotions and endless possibilities from the realm of the living eating her up inside.

It became obvious that Janie was her family's backbone, and that there were some less than ideal factors inhabiting their environment on a regular basis. She was their true shining light and protector, but sadly, now she was gone. But was she gone for good? Were *we* gone for good? It was apparent that that was the only thing on her mind anymore.

"If somehow, in the darkest corner of this fucked up place, there's a path back to my babies, I have to find it… And if standing beside the man who took them away from me can bring me even a half step closer, well then, I guess that'll just be part of my sacrifice."

Her passionate speech and selfless act gave me chills. It validated that all those moments I'd spent dreaming about being with her and conjuring up ideas of who she was as a person, weren't that far off target. Just like I'd done with my parents, I'd created a mock version of her in my head. But the real thing was far more lovely and impressive than I'd imagined.

If I had been less of a coward in my approach to life maybe I could have enjoyed those aspects of her personality when I was alive. She was an incredible woman, with strength, heart, and soul that couldn't be bullied by the darkness. As I gazed into her hazel eyes, I realized I'd finally discovered what love felt like.

I stood up beside her, with a bizarre emotion worming around inside my torso. For the first time in my existence, I suddenly felt like I had a purpose. Even if I couldn't be with Janie, it didn't matter. Above all else I wanted to help. Through hell or high water, if there was a path to get her reconnected with her children, I was going to uncover it.

I turned to Tatiana and Phillip who were both still dejectedly sitting on the fleshy floor. I squinted my eyes at them. There was a fresh motivation stirring inside me.

"Get up. It's time to start moving," I said.

THE TOLL

The tunnel was warm and stagnant. I led the way, stepping into the darkness that was so black it made me feel blind. I pressed my hands against the pulsating walls, feeling my way forward. Each inch I moved increased the amount of fear gnawing on my soul. An impending sensation of doom continued to harp on me, suffocating my senses.

It was hard to determine exactly how long we'd walked. It could have been hours; it could have been days.

Where are we going?
What comes next?
What is the purpose of this journey?

They were all questions that I tried to bury as I walked onward. But to no avail, they continued to resurface in my skull amid the absence of conversation.

I tried not to let the horrors swirling around in my mind dominate me. For the realm we'd entered was clearly the place where nightmares came to manifest, and pleasant daydreams and hope died gruesome deaths.

Suddenly the orangey glow crossed into my vision. The pumpkin-colored tones seemed nefarious in nature, but we had no choice but to venture forward. As best we could figure there was only one path to continue on.

"I think I see something," I said, finally cracking the string of silence.

"What is it?" Tatiana inquired, her words drenched with worry and hesitation.

As I stepped closer to the oval-shaped flesh-gate before me, I could hear blood-curdling moans of absolute agony. The breed of stress leeching onto the terror in a myriad of voices was something hideous. Whatever laid beyond the opening wasn't going to be enjoyable.

A narrow path had finally come into view. The sinister stretch of shaft was about the distance of a football field. It extended over a colossal pit, the likes of which I couldn't yet see the contents of. As I angled in closer, I noticed that the path over the canyon of horror was littered with sharp, shiny spikes that looked metallic. The tangerine tones that illuminated the massive space twinkled off of the rusty steel that lined the pathway.

"It looks like—like some kind of bridge," I replied.

When we stepped through the threshold our bare feet touched down onto the slimy surface before the bridge. This new tissue was tainted; the rotten parts were possessed by the movement of the wicked worms and other various insects found housing in the disgusting architecture.

I stepped closer toward the edge of the platform and looked over into the depths of the pit. Shrieking groans were coming from the countless worms that rolled about and squirmed in the belly of the underpass.

The things below were larger than anything I'd ever seen. They were closer to the outline of an anaconda, mutated to look like something out of a Greek mythology book. The frightening casing harbored a spiny siding similar to a sandworm. Their crude pointed mouths fluttered in waves, comprised of rows and rows of prickly enamel.

"Okay," I said, unsure of what else I could really say about the creepy contents of the pit.

Everyone else carefully made their way to the edges to have a look for themselves. Their expressions told a simple story: no one knew what the fuck to do. The tortures we'd endured up until this point had been forced upon us; we were helpless to avoid them. But this part seemed more about chance than anything. If one of us fell into the worm farm below, I had no idea if we'd ever get out.

"There is only one way we can go," Janie said.

"I agree, but I've gotta wonder, what happens if someone falls? Is that it? Are you just with *them* forever?" I asked, already believing I knew the answer.

"I can't do this!" Tatiana cried.

"Well, unfortunately, I don't think we have much of a choice. I wish there was another way too, but the tunnel led us here," Janie replied.

"We could go back and check again!" Tatiana suggested.

"No! There's nothing back there and you know it! If you want to go back feel free, but I can't waste any more time than I already have. With or without you guys, I'm moving forward," Janie said, turning toward the flooring that made up the jagged, unforgiving bridge.

"Janie, wait!" I yelled. "Let me follow behind you… in case you slip."

Janie nodded and turned forward toward the narrow malignant meat trail. She extended her foot and quickly felt the stabbing pain of the sharp steel tearing into the bottoms of her feet. She expelled guttural screams of profound pain, while I squeamishly watched on. It looked like there were a half dozen fishing hooks setting in deep under her flesh.

I tried to steady her as best I could, and followed up behind. She set her other foot in front of the bloody first and repeated the same wince-inducing impalement. As I watched her try to keep her balance while ripping the twisted steel from her initial step, I felt dizzy thinking about taking my own plunge onto the malevolent metal.

Tatiana looked at Phillip with the eyes of a beggar. "Please, let's go back and see if we can find another way. This is madness! Pure madness!" she cried.

Phillip had been mum on any kind of decision. Neither option probably sounded appealing to him. I was somewhat surprised when he decided to follow in our footsteps and lined up behind me as the bottom of my foot felt the initial anguish of being skewered by rusty barbs.

"We have to move forward," he mumbled.

"You owe me, Phillip! You fucking owe me! You're making a mistake!" Tatiana bellowed.

Phillip didn't answer her back, he was just staring ahead and trying to concentrate like Janie and I.

Tatiana punched the sides of her hips in anger and trotted back to the tunnel of abyss we'd just exited. When she reached the doorway, she looked back at us. Clearly there was some indecisiveness still stewing inside her.

"Fuck all of you!" she yelled.

As the words left her lips the walls started to rumble. The large opening of pink rancid meat that stood before her tightened like an asshole that had finished its shit. Just as Phillip stepped onto the bed of nails walkway, the space that once connected the bridge and platform began to rapidly melt away.

The dripping ruby worm food continued to disappear and draw closer to Tatiana. Horrified screams leapt out of her lungs as the realization struck her; down was the only direction left to travel.

I stopped peeking behind me and focused strictly on what was ahead. Janie pushed on with a soldier's mentality, shredding her feet in the process. I kept my hands on her back trying to both keep her steady and maintain my own balance when the metal began to curl.

The three of us screamed in agony as hunks of steel lodged inside us twisted and curved. The steel was distorting and growing somewhat. To the point where the spears were too bloated and curled for us to dislodge our gory feet.

The magical state of affairs that had once again come to ensnare us was like no trick we would have ever hoped to witness. The bizarre nature we were facing manufactured the most uncomfortable uncertainty. We were dancing with a breed of fright that was groundbreaking.

"What the fuck do we do now?!" Phillip yelled.

Long, endless chains came down from the black sky and attached themselves to the ends of the many pieces of metal that bayonetted us. Suddenly a pair of enormous black hands appeared above. The chains were connected to the mammoth fingers, and as the bridge melted away, we found ourselves dangling upside down at the command of the puppet master.

As the cruel fingertips lowered us down to the worms of wrath, the insane feelings flowing through me became indescribable. I imagined that the same was simmering inside my peers.

There was no talk, only screams.

There was no hope, only horror.

We dangled close enough to watch in detail what was happening to Tatiana, but far enough not to become a part of the vile mayhem.

One of the smaller spiked hellions had devoured her eyeball and burrowed its way into her eye socket. As it chewed its way from the back of her second eye forward, it acted as if it was a weave thread, and Tatiana acted as the blanket of humanity.

A much larger hell worm filled her mouth, forcing her throat to bulge and distend to disturbing dimensions. She flailed about, compelled by cataclysmic trauma, as the largest of the brigade entered her vagina. Her pelvic bones sickeningly cracked and her tissues ripped to accommodate the mammoth devil.

Her pleasure canal split as the evil tube of torment violently twisted its way further. Its beefy exterior pulsated as the tender tissue gave way and the brittle bone splintered. The feminine outline began to distort, a rush of blood giving way as her hole conformed to the wickedness that sought to enter her. The disgusting sight was another to add to the ever-growing list of atrocities that easily superseded even the darkest of memories I'd harbored prior to my demise.

Is this her destiny? I wondered.

Before I could continue my thoughts, we were pulled from the bowels of the worm pit in a flash. I found myself still dangling in sorrow beside both Janie and Phillip. But now we were elsewhere. The rosy walls of pink meat had returned to surround us. The smell of rot invaded my sinus as I regained my focus and zeroed in on the tall being sitting before us.

The throne-like seat was made up mostly of bone and the fleshy framework that always seemed to resurface. The thing sitting in it couldn't be described as a man. While it might have been comprised of a similar blueprint, the additional limbs, discolored surface dominated by rot, and a multitude of thorns that projected out from it, made the thing seem like something dreamed up by an equally abstract and insane mind.

"You must pay the toll," the thorny being explained.

I'm not sure how I heard it because it didn't have a mouth. Somehow the words just happened. Apparently, everyone else heard the same, because Janie, still never losing her sense of urgency amid the madness, was the first to respond.

"The toll for what?" she asked.

"For reentry."

"Will I see my children again?" she asked.

"Perhaps… If you pay the toll."

She tried to shake off some of the drizzling blood that dripped down to her face from her heels and made her naked body look slick in the darkness before continuing.

"Fine. What's the toll?"

"Offer me your most awful memory. Entertain me," the thorn man requested.

Janie's eye's scrunched tight and I could tell this

wouldn't be easy for her. Since our reintroduction, I felt I'd learned that, while on the outside she looked like a bed of roses, things weren't quite as picturesque as I'd once believed.

A white, flashing light suddenly danced off from her forehead and split out into a variety of rays that projected over to a manufactured screen a few yards away from where the disturbing being was seated.

"Are you ready?" he asked, his echoey words finding our skulls telepathically.

Janie nodded. However, it was obvious she was anything but ready. Regardless, the snowy projection of her thoughts found our eyes as we were offered a window into the depravity of her life and times.

The memory began harmless enough. Water flowed from a kitchen sink and we saw what Janie had seen on that day. Dishes were scrubbed and rinsed, but as she stopped the flow of water, we heard crying. The sounds of a baby in grips of discomfort and sadness lingered. Then suddenly, the loud cries cut off.

"What the?" Janie said to herself in the memory.

She raced out of the kitchen and into the bedroom. When the door opened a man held the child over its crib with a look of annoyance and displeasure painted on his face. The baby's body shook back and forth violently. The head whiplashed in horrific fashion, like a car crash being rewound and replayed a handful of times. I watched on in disgust as she tried to stop him. Janie slapped the man in the side of his head quite stiffly. She called him names and screamed in rage. She couldn't believe what she was seeing.

"Let go of her, Paul! You fucking bastard!"

Eventually, he set the baby back down in the crib, but it appeared the damage had been done. The child suddenly looked discombobulated and aloof. Paul looked into the cradle, still somewhat annoyed. The sick son of a bitch was a monster. The type of person that was rotten to the core and only cared about himself.

The thorn man was laughing over the memory. I could see that he truly enjoyed it. Apparently, Janie was giving him exactly what he wanted.

The rest of the memory was even more heartbreaking. It showed some arguments between Janie and Paul. He begged her not to leave him. He said he'd never do it again, it was an accident, any excuse he could think of. He even turned on the tears to pluck at her heartstrings.

The end of the memory was Janie crying as she looked down at her bulging stomach, giving us a hint that she already had another one on the way, compliments of the piece of human garbage Paul.

She was trapped.

I couldn't fault her for trying to continue on with him. She didn't have anywhere else to turn. You invest your entire life into a person, give them your body and soul, create life with them. I'm sure she just didn't want the kids to grow up without a father. How would that benefit them? She was only doing what she thought was right.

I imagined if Paul was abusing his child quietly, he might be abusing her in other ways. I wasn't in a position to judge Janie; I could tell the kind of character that she was comprised of. I felt terrible, but even closer to her now.

"Marvelous," the rotten thorn man said. "Now you," he commanded, pointing his spiked digit toward Phillip.

The white projection lights shifted to Phillip's pale forehead and began to bleed out into our universe. The low-light reel was predictable. Both Janie and I knew that Phillip was scum. We knew what memory he'd be projecting, and the prognostication wasn't wrong.

The images we were seeing felt like they were from a lifetime ago. I used to despise the calibration room, but now I'd give anything to be sitting in it again. We watched Phillip, from his point of view, as he got up from his chair and made his way back to his desk. It was like putting a puzzle together for the first time; we were getting a glance at the slice of slaughter that we hadn't been previously privy to.

He extracted the two guns from his bottom desk draw underneath his coat. After ensuring they were loaded and ready he slowed himself at Janie's desk. There was a picture of her sitting between Bell and Alicia on her desk that Phillip seemed to fixate on.

He tapped the barrel of the gun against the glass and whispered, "Mommy's not coming home today," before expelling a nasty laugh. "Do you know why?"

What? Where the fuck is he going with this? I wondered. It was bizarre to watch him interact and converse with an inanimate object. His brain was clearly not in a traditional headspace.

"Cause Mommy is a stuck-up bitch. Another cunt that doesn't wanna give me the time of day. I'm tired of all the cunts like your mother. Cunts are the reason why I'm alone. If she doesn't wanna give me time, I suppose I'll just have to take it. Take every second that she has left."

I looked over at him, his face had a smile so wide that it bordered on demonic. Janie hung between the two of us and violently thrusted her fist into his lunatic leer. The projection of his memory crackled and was interrupted momentarily.

This enraged the thorn man. A dozen or so of the nauseating spikes that riddled his exterior detached. The pricks launched forward and skewered Janie's hands before plunging deep into her love handles.

She screamed, but still found the will to cuss out Phillip who was re-immersing himself in his fond memory. As more fetid thorns found their way into Janie's upper and lower lips, she had no choice but to be silent and still.

When I looked back at the projection, the memory continued, showing Phillip shooting JC while he sat in his office. It looked like he might have been grazed and hit in the shoulder; none of the bullets appeared to be kill shots, which solved the mystery of why he wasn't wherever the fuck we were.

Phillip was more excited to get back to the calibration

room. The more I watched, the less I thought the shooting was about all the bullshit he'd spewed out when he entered the room. He didn't give a shit about corporate pigs or the evils of the banking industry. That was just his excuse.

He was just another fragile human being with a broken brain. A pathetic story you'd hear in reruns of *Forensic Files*. He'd had his eye set on Janie, just like a lot of people probably did. She was a beautiful and sweet person. But how he could somehow justify her cold-blooded execution was beyond standard comprehension.

Phillip's thoughtful words were a ruse. To paint his life as if it had some kind of purpose before he made his exit. To ensure the pathetic puppy-dog passion wasn't what he'd be remembered for. To propagate a false narrative that would, in the eyes of at least a few imbeciles, make the sacrifice of his life somehow seem righteous.

You're so fucking pointless. This is dumber than I ever imagined. It just doesn't make sense.

Still baffled by the revelation, I struggled to rationalize it. However dumb, it was the reason we were here. My brain continued twisting the Rubik's Cube of hot bullshit trying to make it make sense.

I settled on the notion that with Phillip being quietly obsessed with Janie, in his warped mind, this must've been the only way he could fathom they could be together. Even stranger, he was absolutely right.

As the scene of mass murder played out, I watched Janie's face fall into my lap. I did my best to prevent her from bleeding out. I pressed down on the neck wound as firmly as I could, doing my absolute best to try and keep her alive as long as possible.

The rage festering in her eyes seemed to dip as she digested the end of the vision. When she watched me snatch her off the ruby saturated rug and drag her towards the door. When Phillip pointed the gun at my head and I still turned the handle anyway. When I gave my life without hesitation for an outside chance of saving hers.

I peeped back again, staring at the glossy gratefulness in her eyes. It would've made my knees buckle had I not been hanging from chains and twisted upside down.

Janie didn't blink. I felt permanently entangled with her. However, with the moldy thorns hindering her lips, she couldn't say a word. But she didn't need to. She didn't need to do a thing. We both knew what it was.

Apparently, that wasn't good enough for her though. Janie slowly ripped her gushing limb away from her side. The spikes that pinned her arm down passed through her flesh, and seconds later, her appendage was free.

She reached over and squeezed my hand like she never wanted to let go. Like what I'd done for her meant more than any selfless favor she could've imagined. I could feel the warmth and love transferring from her touch.

Suddenly, another barrage of black needles nailed her hand back to her body. Additional reinforcements were sent into my arm making me cry out before some found my lips as well. I looked back at the sinister being, eyes wide with horror as Phillip's fucked up memory finished with a gunshot to his own cranium.

"ENTERTAIN ME!" it roared.

As the lights warmed my forehead, the memory I never wanted to revisit found its way outside of me. When I watched them project their memories, I thought they had a choice in what they chose to display. Maybe they did, but it certainly didn't feel that way to me.

What filled the projection area was a much younger version of me. It was back at the lonely confines of the orphanage. It began with me watching Billy Reynolds, my best friend at the time, being ushered into a gray Cadillac. Tears left my eyes as I watched the car accelerate slowly from the driveway and disappear down the busy city street.

I wasn't extraordinarily close with Billy. In fact, I'd only known him for about five months. But it was a damn good five months. Probably better than any stretch of time I could recall from my childhood.

Hanging with him was the closest I'd ever been to anyone out of all the years I'd been in that depressing building, and it was the closest I'd ever get. For whatever reason, when potential foster parents visited with me, or looked at me, they looked away and never looked back. It was like there was some kind of invisible stink attached to me.

But one by one, most everyone that came into that place, eventually left to start their lives. Except for me. The ones that remained were the degenerates. Angry and violent damaged goods. I never saw myself in that light, but it didn't matter because the rest of the world did.

The memory continued with me going down to the corner store just moments after Billy left me. I moseyed down to the pharmacy isle and snagged a pair of bottles of Tylenol, discreetly slipping them into my jeans. I bought a 5th Avenue, my favorite candy bar, to avoid suspicion, and fancied it a last meal.

The projection showed me ingesting dozens and dozens of pills in the midnight hour. I passed out in the bathroom on my side. The memory stopped for a moment before abruptly resuming with me throwing up into the toilet. My life was a sad pathetic one. I could feel Janie's eyes on me, more than likely wanting to be there for me, but I was too embarrassed to look at her.

A wave of thunderous laughter erupted from the thorn man. He seemed to take great enjoyment in watching my hardships and the overall pathetic nature of my existence. Finally, he settled down and silence filled the gore chasm.

"You have entertained me sufficiently. Your reentry is complete," he said.

The thorn man stood up from his throne and dissipated into a fine mist. Then the mound of bone and flesh he'd been seated on smoothed away into the surface.

The backdrop of darkness behind the thorn man cleared up, making way for a massive melting pot of humanity. It was an incredible sight to behold. One that most couldn't picture off pure imagination alone.

It was a sea of people, just like us, and they seemed to be doing whatever they pleased. The imagery that had been unleashed was like a carnival of the damned.

Phillip's shackles broke first as the nails in his bloody feet dissolved. He crashed down on his head and quickly stood up. He grabbed each side of Janie's head tightly and started to lick and kiss her disgusted face.

"Get the fuck away from her!" I screamed.

"One way or another, I'm going to have your cunt," he said with a maniacal laugh.

Seconds later, thankfully, my chains gave way and I dropped down just as he was finishing his warped threat.

Phillip took off running as best he could, despite his limp from the gaping holes in his feet.

"You fucking scum!" I yelled beginning to chase him.

But as I watched him vanish into the awful ocean of blasphemous humanity, I thought better of it. I returned to Janie whose chains had also finally broken. The thorn man had left us, but his minions still remained.

I used my free hand to pull the decaying ebony needles from her arms. Once they were free, they bled generously, but she still helped extract the thorns from my side. It felt like a mad race to remove them all as I pulled the final spike from her lip. At first I thought it was just the excitement of removing the foreign object that was lodged inside her, but I quickly realized that wasn't the motivation when she pounced on top of me and pressed her bloody lips against mine.

I didn't mind that she tasted like blood. As her tongue entered my mouth, I just stroked the side of her head like I'd never touched anyone before. I was home now. We were home now.

THE NEW NORMAL

The sex was incredible, in part because it was the first time I didn't have to pay when it was all said and done, but mostly because I'd never made love to someone that I had feelings for. For the first time I felt a connection, not just an erection. It was electrifying. I wish it wasn't as bloody as it was, but the love in my ribcage was all that mattered. It was a thing of beauty.

The sludgy crimson continued to pour from the wounds in her arm and torso while I thrusted deep inside her. My tongue flailed passionately around the gaping holes left by the thorns above and below her lips. The irony taste of leaking hot blood didn't stall me, instead it fueled me. I wanted to feel connected to Janie's inner, most personal, biology. Her body and mine truly becoming one.

This impossible moment of ecstasy made me feel like I'd been bound to the celluloid of some wicked lost film. It had to be fantasy, yet, it wasn't. The sudden realization that an outlandish, and admittedly gorier, connection I'd day-dreamt about during the countless Groundhog Days at my desk, had finally manifested, was almost more than I could handle.

As Janie's slick, self-lubricated entrance applied pressure to my erection, I could see she was overwhelmed by our bond too. We were a pair of magnets now; I felt an infinite gushing attraction that I was sure could never cease.

Janie laid in my arms for hours. Her previously hurried state somehow paused after our embrace as we watched the utter chaos of the new world that had been shown to us. Nothing could dampen the moment, not even the slew of bizarre and repulsive acts that the human traffic shamelessly displayed.

It was like watching a parade of madness; the world we'd descended into was a place run by lunatics. I suppose it wasn't much different than before, but the people just didn't have the decency to pretend here.

As I watched a pair of men smashing their heads together, in a strange way it was refreshing. The bloody brows and loud cracking of skulls would have normally disturbed me. But as I noticed the smiles on both their faces I thought, *At least they're genuine.*

Another woman sat holding a baby. Moments later she struck it in the face and then stood up and spiked it on the ground like a wide receiver after a touchdown. She didn't stop there; she continued to stomp and kick the tiny thing relentlessly. Then once the head was bloody, she slowed, laying down on the ground beside it.

The disturbed gal proceeded to insert her fingers into her vagina.

Then her fist...

Then her forearm...

Where the devil is this going? I wondered. *These people aren't right*.

I looked over at Janie who appeared to be watching the same thing. Strangely enough she looked somehow stoic. I wasn't expecting to see such blankness, but nonetheless, there it sat.

I didn't have to wait long to understand what the sick woman had in mind. She continued her chaos on the ground. The repeated in and out got her pussy so wide, that pushing the blood-drenched child's skull into her opening was hardly a chore at all. We watched as she laid out, commencing a reverse birth, suffocating what was left of the gasping baby's bloody face.

"How does a fucking child go to hell? I mean what could he have possibly done?" I wondered aloud.

"It doesn't make sense," Janie stammered.

"It's fucking insane out there," I whispered.

"I know. Is it strange that, for some reason, it doesn't bother me?" Janie asked sheepishly.

"It's the damnedest thing, isn't it? I thought it was just me. What have they done to us?"

"Desensitization I suppose."

"It's funny you say that."

"Why?"

"Because, there was a thing… a face in the darkness that spoke to me before our paths crossed. It was right when I came in, after Phillip shot me in the head. I don't know what prompted me really, maybe it was just morbid curiosity. But as it continued to shred my body, I was able to ask why it was hurting me."

"What did it say?"

"It said… to prepare you."

"Prepare you? Prepare you for what?"

"Well, that's exactly what I asked." I almost didn't want to say it but I owed it to Janie to share what I'd learned.

"And?"

"It said it was preparing me for eternity."

Janie suddenly shot upward to her feet.

"Hey, what are you doing?" I asked.

She continued staring, even more deeply now, at the baby suffocating on the woman's snatch. Something had clicked in her head. The strange comfort we'd found ourselves nestled warmly together in was shattered. A fear filled her eyes as she thought about the notion. I could tell that Bell and Alicia were on her mind. She slowed for a moment and let the adrenaline settle.

"I don't want to discount or take away from anything that just happened. I fucking love you, Andy. I wish I had gotten to know you before, but better late than never, I guess," she said, letting a kind smile cross her face.

"Well, this is about as fucking late as it gets," I replied.

She laughed, looking so damn cute when she did. I had to inject a little humor into the situation; it just felt so utterly hopeless.

"But I suppose I love you too," I said with a charming grin. It might've been the first time I'd smiled since my murder.

"What you did for me, that meant everything. You sacrificed everything to—to try and save me. To try and get me back to my daughters."

"Well, I didn't exactly have a lot going on, but… I'm glad I did, because, as fucked up as it might sound, I'd do it again in a heartbeat."

Janie kissed me again. I didn't think she could do it with any more passion than she'd done before, but she found a way. Our hearts touched, and even though they weren't beating, I knew they were in sync.

I could taste the guilt on her tongue when she finally tore her lips away from mine and refocused. The fresh love had blinded her momentarily, but I could tell now her mortal absence was weighing on her. I'm sure in the back of her head, the whole time she'd been wondering if that fucking psycho Paul was 'getting annoyed' again.

"I have to know," she explained.

"Know what?" I asked.

Janie's expression became dead-serious. The eternal drive that I'd witnessed when we crossed the barbed bridge and been forced to offer our darkest horrors to the thorn man resurfaced with a vengeance. Embers in her eyes, rabid determination on her face.

"If there's a way to see my children."

Suddenly I felt my manner and posture matching Janie's. My love for her and all we'd been through raged. We were in this together to the end. Or to no end if what the monster in the sky said was accurate.

"If there's a way, I promise you, Janie, we'll find it."

***

When we crept out of the darkness our surroundings became more alien with each step. The mass of mankind was so thick and widespread it looked like a disease. I told Janie we should hold hands at all times. If we got separated, it seemed possible that we might never be able to reconnect.

The twisted thought played over in my head. Knowing that the person you loved more than anything was in the same place, but you might spend an eternity in search of them. We needed to make sure that would never happen. All we had was each other.

We didn't know where to begin. The majority of the hordes of people seemed to be possessed by their desires. Demonic dancing, gruesome orgies, and ghastly acts of extreme violence surrounded us from every angle.

The people looked just like we did; normal. From all walks of life and from all parts of the globe. They were inviting with their activities but not forceful. For the most part, the majority seemed to have willing bodies ready to partake in just about anything and everything that the imagination could draw up.

We wanted information but the chaos was intimidating. We had no idea how to approach the excess inebriated sinners. We were looking for someone who didn't seem like they fit in. Someone who didn't appear stark-raving mad. It felt like we had been sifting through the wickedness for hours, but we never found that person. Instead, he found us.

"You two look a little lost, are you new around here?" a high-pitched voice inquired from behind us.

When Janie and I turned around, our sights were met with a tiny, obese man. His beady brown eyes came up to about my nipples and the top of his head was balding. His pencil thin mustache was thin across the center but twisted at both ends. Gray hairs blended into the curly black ones and his plump gut draped over his pubic region. His smile was friendly enough, but disturbing in its own way. The odd fellow was clearly an adult but had somehow retained his baby teeth, a not too uncommon deformity.

The tarnished canary-colored chiclets began to move again. "The name's Fink," the trollish man said, extending his hand.

The offering of a handshake was about the most normal thing since I could remember. I quickly obliged him, happy to communicate with someone that wasn't acting in a murderous manner.

"I'm Andy and this is Janie," I said, locking palms with his grubby hand.

"The pleasure's all mine. I can always tell when there's a newbie in the ranks."

"How did you know?"

"Well, you're not bored yet. You see all this?" he asked, gesturing to the storm of perversion and decadence that surrounded us.

Janie and I both nodded as if to say 'of course, how could we miss it?'

"This is what boredom looks like."

"How long have you been down here?"

"Long enough that even all this no longer interests me," he said with a chuckle.

"Where are we?" Janie interjected.

"That's quite the question. I'd love to help you, I really would. I remember in the beginning, I had so many questions. It took me centuries to understand it. I had to scavenge high and low, talk to millions of people to put the pieces together. But you see," he lifted his fat fingertips and twisted one of the ends of his mustache mischievously, "that kind of information isn't free. Centuries worth of hard work can't just be handed out for nothing. That's criminal."

He was building to something; I could tell he wanted to barter. But what could he want? I supposed an even better question was, what did we have to give?

"So, what do you propose?" Janie was speaking with a sense of urgency. Clearly the girls were still on her mind, but I didn't want the little goblin man to take advantage of us. He didn't seem like he truly aimed to help. He seemed to have an agenda.

"Why don't we get away from all this bedlam and talk. If we can work out a deal then, I promise, I'll tell you anything you want to know."

Janie couldn't resist the shortcut. Time was of the essence and we had no idea how much had passed. In her mind there was no other option, we needed to go with Fink.

She looked up at me with her enchanting eyes and nodded. Without hesitation, I bobbed my head in agreement. She would do anything to obtain the answers.

"Okay, let's go," she said.

"Wonderful," Fink replied, grinning ear to ear.

EVIL ENTERTAINMENT

It took us a few hours to arrive at Fink's lair. The further we walked the more anxiety crept up inside me. Apparently, we weren't immune to nervousness in death. But after some time, I actually began to feel more comfortable. The route he'd taken us down must've been a seldom used one.

The vast overpopulation observed where we'd found ourselves initially, seemed inescapable, yet Fink had found a way around it. This detail led me to lend more credence to the notion he might actually have the information he boasted about.

The area we roamed was now barren, and a short distance away sat a mountain of the pink fleshy tissue with an abundance of misshapen teeth wedged inside it. Some long, some dull, some sharp, some decaying, some massive. It was a peculiar sight, but incredible in its own way.

More often than not, I found myself being amazed by the many surreal sights. As disgusting and extraterrestrial as much of it was, the shock value seemed to be fading. It was all so special, so fantastic. I felt excitement swelling inside me. Our questions would soon be answered.

At the bottom of the molar mountain, Fink approached a sharp and particularly yellow incisor. It was smaller than the others that were plainly visible from hundreds of yards away. He looked behind him sneakily, as if to be sure no one was watching. He then placed his sausage fingers around the edges of the softball-sized tooth and twisted it slightly to the left.

A small patch in the side of the gummy mountain began to part, creating a small opening in the structure that at first glance looked completely solidified. Once we breeched the hole it closed up behind us.

"Right this way," Fink said, gesturing toward a wet magenta box that was fixed to the side of the wall.

Once inside, he approached a wall covered in various teeth and tapped a few pieces of enamel. As the box elevated upward, Fink rolled his eyes, then looked at us and said, "One of the things that gets old quick about this place is you have to fucking walk everywhere."

When the cell of meat came to a halt, we were much higher up than I'd thought. The mountain of meat was butted up against a vast pit. Fink's living quarters were comprised in such a way that you could look out into the endless flesh-scape and so much farther.

The housing was far more impressive than we imagined from a man of his stinky stature. There were some different sitting areas that looked almost like couches, chairs and a table. They were comprised of various tongue-like tissue and, of course, more teeth.

"This is nice," I said, not believing what I was saying.

"Thanks. The teeth take a little while to get used to, but I call it home. Believe it or not, something like this is a premium space," Fink explained.

"Oh, I'd believe just about anything at this point," I replied with a friendly wink.

"You ain't kidding," Fink said, plopping down on the squishy wet sofa. "Please, have a seat."

Both Janie and I plopped down on the squishy couch variety of meaty seating across from him. It felt good to rest my heels. They still hadn't quite healed properly from the earlier incident of violence.

"Once you've been around here long enough, everything you saw, the anarchy, it just gets a little dated. You'll start searching for things that you never really thought about too much when you were alive. Things like quiet and isolation. However, I don't want to seem as if I don't partake. I most certainly did, for quite some time. But like anything it can get old. You have to evolve quite a bit here before you can reach that tier of enlightenment."

"Forgive me if I seem direct, but I have a time sensitive issue that I'm trying to address, and learning these little nuggets of truth that you're offering out of the kindness of your heart I appreciate. But would it be too forward to ask you if I'm allowed to ask a question? And if not when would it be appropriate?"

Janie was so intelligent and polite, especially when she was motivated. She knew how to get the ball rolling without offending the party she required assistance from.

"Understood, I can certainly appreciate your honesty and urgency. I know what it's like to be new. There's a million things you need to know and you need to know them right away," Fink said, stroking his mustache with his dirty fingers once again.

"I think you'd be able to ask your questions pretty quickly. Maybe in just a few minutes even. But first, as previously discussed, the two of you will need to do a little something for me," Fink said brandishing his bizarre baby teeth. "And, to help you better understand, let me ask you a question."

"Please," Janie replied.

"What don't you see here?" he asked, pointing around the walls of his home.

"People?" Janie replied.

"Well, we're people now, aren't we? Try again."

I could see Janie was a little aggravated by the guessing game. I wanted to help before she got pissed and ended up offending the strange man. I pondered the query a little bit more, then suddenly, it struck me; the answer was obvious.

"Everything," I said.

"Bingo, the exact opposite of your answer my dear. There's no cups, no food, no toys, no games. The only thing we have here is flesh and bone. Therefore, the only feasible currency in this realm is simple. It's entertainment. It's all entertainment. And you'll soon learn that people run out of ideas pretty fast here, so when you finally have a good one, there's nothing more exciting than bringing it to life. It's all we have really. So, now that you understand, I'd like you to entertain me," Fink said, letting his hand slowly stroke the epic tooth beside him.

"Okay, that sounds easy enough," Janie said, looking over at me. "I supposed we can do that…"

"Wonderful!" he giggled mischievously before corralling his glee to continue. "But I must forewarn you, the variety of concepts that are brought to light here are rather extreme. It all may seem like madness and depravity, but afterwards, when I answer your questions, you'll grasp it better. I don't want to seem too forward in my request, but it's simply the way things are here."

Janie and I both listened carefully to Fink as he tried to sell and justify whatever weirdness he was about to suggest. The notion made me highly uncomfortable, but we had no other option but to nod suspiciously.

"So, I had a thought which, ironically, I just recently recalled some hours ago. I was among the other heathens some time ago and the subject of gum-jobs came up. Are you familiar with those?"

We both looked at each other, I didn't want to say it, but

it just came out. "Is that like when an old lady without teeth gives a guy a blowjob?"

"Precisely!" Fink bellowed with excitement.

Janie shot me a sideways look, almost disappointed I knew what the disturbed troll was talking about.

Fink was so fired up that I understood the concept, that his big belly jiggled with joy. I couldn't help but glance at the tip of his tiny pecker peeking out just below the doughy flab. We had been naked so long that the nudity felt normal now, but I dreaded that his measly manhood would somehow be involved.

"But as you can see, we don't have an old lady here," Fink continued. "The age at which we die at is the age that we remain. So, Andy, what I'd like to see happen is for you to beat the teeth out of Janie's pretty little mouth and then allow her to go down on you. If you think you can do that, then we can move right on to your questions."

The sick little shit sounded like a used car salesman. The way he just sort of slipped fucked up shit in there real quick and tried to get you to sign on the dotted line.

The idea horrified me, but in a way, I was relieved that he didn't want to defile her. I still didn't want to hit Janie; she'd been through enough. We'd just professed our love to each other a short while ago. I could never hurt her, no matter what the cause might be. Amid the awkward silence, the little man continued trying to sell us on the idea.

"Ever since I've been living around all these damn teeth, I just… I just can't stop thinking about them. I need to see it, and because I'm more of the private type these days, I won't just invite anyone into my home. But I'm a people watcher, we all are in here, and I can tell that the two of you are no trouble. You've both just reentered, with so many mysteries of your own to unravel. It's a perfect trade-off really. If you make it happen, I'll give you everything. I'm talking the Holy Grail of info. I'll save you centuries."

The plump little fucker's man-boobs jiggled sloppily with anticipation as his tiny, frozen heart awaited the response. I looked at Janie for counsel. I wasn't going to be the one to say yay or nay. I had nothing on my agenda.

There was no one I needed to get in touch with. No one that I felt detached from. No normalcy that I yearned for. The past was just that for me. I left the ball in her court but found myself shaking my head in disgust.

"Just do it," Janie said with a cold look stewing in her pupils.

"Janie… I can't," I replied.

From the corner of my eye, I studied Fink. His tiny teeth ground against each other back and forth with a perverse enthusiasm. Was gorging on my apprehensive discomfort part of his evil entertainment? Was this why he liked newbies?

"Andy, it's okay. I need you to do it. I need to find out where we go from here. Like he said, the pain is temporary. My teeth will grow back."

"They will!" Fink echoed twirling his mustache around.

I couldn't believe I was about to knock her fucking teeth out. I'd never so much as punched a person, let alone a girl… that I loved. But I knew more than anything this was what she wanted—no, what she needed. It was all part of the sacrifice.

"How should I do it? With my hands?" I asked.

"You might actually be better served using your heel or knee," Fink interjected, graciously offering his own twisted perspective.

Janie looked at him and then back at me. "I'm assuming he knows from experience. I guess I can just lay down on the floor and you can take it from there."

She elevated herself off the fleshy seating and laid her body flat against the gum-like material. Janie pulled her lips and smiled big. It was such an enchanting beam of sunshine. The last thing I wanted to do was destroy it, but I had no choice.

I sent the point of my heel crashing into her teeth with as much force as I could muster. I didn't want to watch, but

I had to keep my eyes open and ensure I didn't miss the intended target.

As my calcified body crashed into her happiness, I watched a few of the pearly whites crack. I had used enough force and accuracy to blast out Janie's front teeth on the first connection, while also cracking a couple on her lower jaw.

Janie started to choke as they tumbled down her throat. She turned sideways and spit pieces up, along with a sizable amount of blood.

"YESSSS!" Fink bellowed. "Again! Get them all out! All of them!"

I could see the pain on her face. I was responsible. It made me feel less than human. But through the anguish and violence, Janie remained strong. Her dollish glossy eyes looked up at me before she laid back down again. Through her broken grin and swollen lips, she spoke.

"Like he said, Andy, don't stop this time. Just get it over with, please."

She was so fucking strong. I knew I had to be strong for her too. I had to stomach the depravity without flinching, otherwise it would only elongate the process for her.

I raised my foot back up and brought it down full force, targeting the side of her jaw this time. Once I connected, I immediately heard more cracking. I started my motion again and nailed the other side equally hard.

There was a stinging pain in my foot, so I transitioned my onslaught. Dropping the full weight of my body down, I vaulted knee first, bulling my stiff cap into her entire orifice. The broken and fragmented enamel sliced around my kneecap, but the force and weight loosened a few more of her teeth. I made my way back to my feet again, and launched another pair of rapid heel strikes before thinking that I needed to assess the damage.

A river of blood was now exiting Janie's mouth from all directions. She turned slowly to her side, still clearly stunned from the beating. It was like a big mixing bowl filled with blood and teeth had just been poured out all over the floor.

I bent down and looked at her lips and gums. "I'm sorry. I'm so sorry," I confided, caressing her clumpy hair.

Most of the teeth aside from the molars were gone entirely, but a few had been broken off and remained jagged and almost creature-like.

"Please, Fink, is this enough?! You can see nearly all of her upper and lower gums. I don't know how I'd get the one in the back out without some sort of device," I pleaded.

The bulbus little bastard stroked his whiskers again thoughtfully. "Alright, I suppose. But it's only because I really do enjoy the two of you."

I didn't know whether to say thank you or fuck you. So, I remained silent. I lifted Janie up back onto the squishy sofa and sat beside her. Her jaw was slacked, exposing the fresh damage I'd done, as well as the heavy blood flow leaking from the deep red holes where her teeth had been.

"Now, for the true spectacle," Fink mumbled rubbing his ballooned hands together.

Janie was still quite out of it, but not so much so that she didn't remember what came next. When the hot bleeding gum-tissue connected with my cock, I thought I might be sick. But I don't think there was a way to be sick anymore.

Shitting, pissing, vomiting, and blowing my nose all seemed like forgotten functions. Yet whomever created the rules where we were trapped, thought it reasonable to leave bleeding, drooling, and cumming on the table still. It seemed like that's all people did in Hell.

The sex we'd enjoyed earlier was bloody, but different than the oral variety that was beginning to transpire between us. We didn't have a Rumpelstiltskin look-a-like ogling over us. I hadn't just mashed her vagina to a pulp. The entire thing was surreal and disturbing.

Yet, as it went on, my cock only got harder. The wet hot bleeding hole I'd created felt strangely wonderful. As she gagged and pushed it into the back of her throat, I could feel the tiny broken tips of her teeth scraping along my shaft. Not only was I starting to enjoy it, Janie was becoming more animated too.

I grabbed onto a clutter of Janie's gory hair, feeling myself rumbling with ecstasy. As the load of gunky white fluid erupted from my mushroom tip, Janie put her busted and swollen lips against the base of my balls, happily receiving and swallowing the orgasm in its entirety.

When she lifted her head off my crotch, I couldn't help but feel bad still. Seeing her face ruined and ravaged brought me back to the pain I'd inflicted upon her. It was something I never wanted to be associated with, but the twinkle in her eyes comforted me. It looked past the mayhem that I administered and was one of love and understanding.

As the blood married with my ejaculation dribbled out of her mashed opening, she held my hand and looked over at Fink. He sat projecting a dramatic slow clap, with some ejaculation of his own splattered over his puffy gut.

"Excellent. Now, since you've thoroughly entertained me, I *really* want to help the two of you. So, as promised, the floor is all yours. Ask away," he said with a quick wink.

Janie tried to speak but her jaw was flopping and the words weren't quite coming together. I think I knew what she wanted to get at right away. I put my hand on her soft shoulder and spoke on her behalf. But I felt there were a few initial questions we needed to get answered before what she was thinking.

"Is this Hell?" I asked.

"I can see why you might think that. The short answer is no," Fink explained.

"Well, give me the long answer then. What is… all this?" I asked, pointing around the room and out toward the masses of disturbed beings that could be seen far off in the distance wreaking havoc on each other.

"The better question would be, what *are we*? I suppose the best way to describe this place is eternity. We are a melting pot of personality, color, ideas, and linguistics. Upon your reentry, you saw them, yes?"

"We saw many things. The worms. The faces. Pure

abomination."

"The myriad of deformities are just tools at their disposal, creations to torture and instill fear. But did you see the mouthless men comprised of black flesh and thorns?"

"Yes, that was the last thing we saw before being left here."

"What they are actually called cannot be pronounced, but around here we refer to them as Thorns."

"Because of their skin?"

"Sure, and there is a metaphorical meaning, I suppose. They are the thorns in our side, the controllers of eternity. The terms always seemed two-fold to me."

"What are they?"

"They are another species, just like us. I'm sure you noticed some of their traits are quite similar to ours but not exactly. We are, of course, far more limited and tender. Intentionally limited, one might suspect."

"But why?"

"You still haven't figured it out? I thought you might have. I alluded to it somewhat before. Throughout the existence of mankind, the lone nagging question has always been there: what is our purpose?"

I was hanging on the edge of my seat, I had no idea where he was going with it, but he was right. It's the most coveted question in all of history.

"The answer may be a bit lackluster. At least I thought it was."

I was going to fucking explode if he strung me along any further.

Fink diddled his mustache again before continuing, "But sadly, we are all just entertainment."

"What?"

"Our entire species is just something to observe for a giggle or gasp here and there."

"That's the most insane thing I've ever heard."

"Why is that? You're up to speed on current society. People that are alive right now have done the same. Kind of ironic that the species created as entertainment would evolve so much, that it would eventually seek its own endless flavors of it."

"I don't understand."

"C'mon, you've seen it! You lived through it! Don't play stupid. We've gone forward in a way like never before. We've completely repackaged ourselves into these never-ending, ludicrous limelight specials. We produce bizarre reality shows, sing ridiculous songs, and tell inflammatory jokes. It's all merely entertainment. Our mortal lives are just a constant series of distractions. But here it's different."

Fink's grin began to fade. His demeanor became serious.

"In this realm where there is no disease, death, or famine, boredom is the number one killer. Some time ago, the Thorns weathered a great depression. A philosophical illness that spanned the entire spectrum of their species, infecting the absolute brightest to the bottom feeders. It is a question that the greater populous sought to answer, but remained unaccounted for over many millennia. The same one we humans constantly search to crack. What the fuck are we doing? Why are we here?"

I looked back a Janie momentarily. Her gory face was engrossed in the conversation. As I watched her eyes continue to bulge, I felt comfort in her presence. I knew she had other questions that were personally more pressing, but I was glad she wasn't blinded by just those thoughts.

"And so, century after century, disappointment after disappointment, the pressure grew. Would that same gnawing thought harass them forever? That seemed to be the case, and rather than wait around for eons, they decided they wanted to know sooner. Death was the only option outside of utter redundancy. And so, this realization, or lack thereof, fostered a tsunami of suicides. This nasty rash of self-annihilations infected these power-drunk, otherwise immortal beings, nearly extinguishing the Thorns as a whole. Imagine that… knowing that you'll live forever, but having nothing in your world captivating enough to keep you from cashing out."

Fink had no way of knowing, but on a smaller level, I understood it. Back when I was alive there wasn't a whole lot keeping me going. Thoughts of jumping off a bridge or getting a gun surfaced in my skull on more than one occasion. And even in pondering it during those moments, I came to the sick realization that, in a fucked-up way, death was the best thing to ever happen to me.

"So, with the Thorns having been confronted by this giant crisis, there was a forced evolution. During this dark period, the surviving members of their scientific community convened to brainstorm. Long story short, they decided that the cure-all would be finding a way of occupying their minds. If they were distracted, they wouldn't become so cynical. If their brains were constantly engaged elsewhere then they needn't worry about the philosophical death-inducing disease. Maybe the more astute thinkers still wouldn't be swayed, but, if they could sort of keep themselves asleep while remaining conscious, overall, this would ensure their survival. And so, *we* came to exist."

"Wait, so, we're—we're all just some kind of social experiment?"

"A quite successful one. During all those moments when you might've thought your life had no purpose, really, it did. You were saving lives and didn't even know it."

"How'd they—I mean, shit." So many thoughts were racing through my skull. I felt overwhelmed. It was hard to figure out what to ask next. "Were we just grown, or—or developed in a lab?"

"The creation aspects are quite technical. I've had it broken down to me hundreds of times, yet still, it remains almost beyond explanation."

"Okay... Well, what—what about Heaven? How can you explain—"

"It's just a lights and mirror show. It's all a façade, a pretty carrot to dangle in front of mankind and help keep humanity motivated. You've probably heard about those images of light and beauty that people see upon having a near death experience."

I nodded. Those recollections were the first thing I thought about when I was traveling through the darkness.

"Equate it to special effects. Projected images, illusions, fog machines, but don't discount it. From what I hear those guys have a hell of a time keeping up with it all. It's a full-time job for many of the Thorns."

"Jesus," I muttered to myself.

"He was real, but just a regular guy. You might call him a conman even. But you shouldn't be too shocked coming from the world you were plucked from. They kind of hit the nail on the head with the whole simulation theory. It's not exactly that, but pretty much. For me it was much harder to comprehend. I was a casualty of the Hundred Years War. It took me centuries to learn about all these new evolutions. I wasn't bullshitting you when I said I've spoken with millions. Aside from talking there isn't much else to do around here but fight and fuck. But imagine that, a simple medieval mind like mine having to keep up with all this. I think I've done a decent job. Kept up with current events, technology improvements, and learned nearly every language. I had to in order to satisfy my quest for information."

"Entertainment." I was still just speechless, sort of reliving the ideas over again and trying my best to absorb them as truth.

"Yup. That's why upon reentry they keep the blood and cum active. Pain and pleasure we're still allowed to toy with during this static phase. It was a gift from the Thorns."

"Well, I understand pleasure… but pain seems a bit cruel to allow."

"That's because you don't understand the Thorns fully. You see, existence is far different than what we've been told. Happiness isn't actually real, it's just a creation. Something that was volleyed into the universe to further their amusement. Over time, it just warped our perspective."

"How so?"

"It sounds more than a little strange when you hear it for the first time, but in the Thorns' world, it's pain and violence that are revered. Think of it like this, did you ever watch horror movies when you were alive?"

"All the time."

"I wish that fucking stuff existed when I was alive; it sounds so badass. Nonetheless, I have a grasp of what they represent. I'm told that when people watch horror movies, they actually get a rise out of the murders in them. Some people watch for the kills alone. Something that they would be totally traumatized by in real life is accepted in fantasy. Yet somehow, they find a way to adore being disgusted and horrified by whatever nastiness the creator of such entertainment can concoct."

"Okay…" I didn't know where he was going with it.

"It's just backwards with the Thorns. This wart on the brain of man… this happiness and sunshine… it's like watching a horror movie to them. Except they don't wince and cringe when the murders are happening, they wince and cringe when people get married or take care of their sick mothers or adopt a child. It's utterly repulsive to them, but like us, they eat that shit up."

"What the fuck… it's all backwards. This is heavy, heavier than I would've ever imagined."

"But wait, then you have the other side of the coin. They also like to see what they love. Just like people enjoy a good comedy or heartfelt story, they want it too. That's why you have things like death, cold sores, alcohol. It's literally just a bunch of the Thorns in the creative department, sitting at a table and thinking this shit up. Then boom! They pop the idea into one of our heads and unleash the beast. Alcohol, that one brings even an old fart like me back. It's just brilliant. Give people something that's addictive and that they enjoy, but if they have too much, it'll kill them, and probably others too. HIV is also one that's pretty genius. Kill us through sex! That'll sure as hell speed up your reentry."

Fink was getting really excited discussing the dark architecture of humanity. I found it comical on one hand, but on the other I felt cold and sinister speaking about it so openly. My mind was beginning to reshape as all the answers to life's greatest queries continued to circulate. Maybe I shouldn't have been feeling callous and disgusted. It was all just some illusion, wasn't it? I had most likely been programmed to evoke these emotional responses, but did that make it wrong?

"You keep mentioning reentry. What do you mean by that?" It seemed like an important term to understand.

"I call it reentry because we were created here, so we're coming back, right?"

"Why do you come back with the people that you die with? Is that always the case?"

"It is if you die together. If you die together, you come in together. If you die alone, you come alone. The Thorns find it interesting to pair people up in that manner. They really enjoy watching people work together and against each other. At least that's what I've been told."

"So, we're just here now… forever?"

"Most likely."

"What do you mean most likely?"

"Well, have you looked at your tongue yet?"

"Noooo," I said sarcastically.

Fink stuck out his beefy tongue. Printed on the top of the slimy muscle was a massive number; one so lengthy that I couldn't count the digits.

"Nobody alive knows we have them, but we're all being tracked. They show back up upon reentry."

"What do they mean?"

"Think of it like a barcode, I guess. Every person is unique. They use these for the lottery."

"Lottery? What do you get if you win?"

"It's not like that… nobody *wins* this lottery."

"Well, why—" Janie nudged me in the arm and used her

other hand to lift her jaw up to her face. She held it together as best she could and attempted to speak again. We'd really gone down a rabbit hole, I felt bad about not bringing up Janie's children earlier.

"Is there a way to talk and visit people that are still alive?" she asked in her ghastly tone as blood continued to pour from her face.

"Visit and talk, no. But if you wanted to see them… there is one way. For me it's irrelevant. I can't really find a use for it. Once in a great while I will, just out of morbid curiosity. To see how things have changed. Everyone I knew in the 1300s is already down here somewhere for the most part," Fink explained.

"But could *we* use it?" Janie asked, slurping and slurring her annunciation.

"I suppose you could, but it's far away from here. It'll be quite a walk. I wouldn't do this for just anyone… but I'll bring you, if you'd like," Fink replied.

I could tell by the look in Janie's dry eyes that the idea gave her hope. However small, there was still hope.

A BROKEN THORN

It felt like we'd taken a billion steps. The land looked similar to everything else; tissue-like and moist. I was grateful that the path was mostly deserted. I had no idea how Fink could keep track of such a route. I didn't ask, but the creepy little man hadn't bluffed us. He'd delivered on all of his boasts and promises thus far.

"Why aren't there any people out this way?" Janie asked. Her jaw had finally healed and her teeth were coming in again.

"Mostly boredom. Everyone is usually busy keeping themselves entertained in the present. Once you've been here awhile, you don't much have use for the past. Also, not just anyone knows about Belthorn. You have to be at it awhile, like me, to know," Fink replied.

"What's Belthorn?" I asked.

"Not what, but who. Belthorn is one of the Thorns, hence the name. He lives among the human populous, which is extremely odd."

"Why is it odd?" Janie asked.

"Because they're segregated. They have their own haven. You don't think it would be strange to live with a sub-species that you created?"

"I guess," Janie said.

"The combination would be utter chaos!" Fink yelled.

We were walking into an eerie, hot wind. It created a whipping noise that left us increasing our pitch to hear each other.

"Is he the only one?" I asked.

"There may be more. He's the only one I'm aware of. We're quite lucky he's here, much of the knowledge I've accumulated over time about the Thorns was directly from him. Without him, I'm sure I'd still be wondering what the hell the point of all this is."

I looked past Fink and out toward the bizarre backdrop. "How can it be real?" I mumbled to myself, still having difficulty grasping the strange nature of my journey.

"This space seems endless at times. I've often wondered how far it stretches. There are moments when I feel like an ant in the desert," Fink said, turning back and letting out a snicker.

"Why is he here? Why did this Belthorn leave his own society?" Janie wondered aloud.

"Every society has its outcasts. From what I heard, they thought he was a little too much like us."

Finally, in the distance, I took in a sight that wasn't just bare bumpy land and hills. There was something and it was moving. As we closed in, I came to realize the motion I'd been fixed on was derived from an enormous ocean of a thick scarlet substance. *Is it blood?* I wondered.

When we reached the shores I saw, far out in the fluid, a small island that appeared to be comprised of the pinkish, fleshy material that we'd come to know so well.

"I hope you're up for a swim," Fink said glancing over at Janie and I.

As we looked out into the violent crimson tide, part of me thought the same thing I always did when entering any water outside of a bathtub or swimming pool; the unknown is an endless bucket of fear. The single thing we are most disturbed by as humans.

"Is there anything we should know about swimming around in there?" I asked.

A loud crack of thunder let loose in the gloomy sky. I had yet to notice it, but there were clouds above us.

I should've known the rain would be red, yet, somehow, it still surprised me. As the claret secretion trickled down our faces, Fink grinned again and finally looked prepared to answer my query.

"What's it matter? You can't die anymore," he said with a chuckle, then plunging into the plasma pool.

"But we can still feel pain!" I yelled.

Janie did exactly what I expected her to do. She shrugged her shoulders and kissed me on the lips.

"Maybe it's better we don't know," she said before diving in after Fink.

"Goddamnit," I mumbled, although that expression had seemed to lose its relevance of late.

The 'water' was as warm and thick as it looked from the shoreline. If felt like I was wafting through curdled milk; the distinct differences being that the texture of the ocean I was accustomed to took far less work, and I could see what was swimming around me.

We swam for what felt like forever without issue. The feeling wasn't getting any less creepy, but I was happy it was only mildly uncomfortable. I was beginning to feel a bit tired, but I powered forward, using Janie's motivation as my fuel. It wasn't until we were a couple hundred yards from reaching the island when it happened.

The blood growled and bubbled aggressively only a short distance away from us. The gunky fluid parted as an enormous figure broke through. It towered over us, reaching skyscraper measurements at first glance.

The thing's snout was thick and hairy. The elongated tube-like nose stretch down so far it nearly reached us. The nostrils and mouth were so close to each other that they were nearly joined. The body was muscular and covered in a leathery black skin, while the shoulders and rim of its torso were fuzzy but matted from the gnarly fluid it had been previously submerged in. The three fingers on each of its hands were meaty, and they opened and closed nonstop like a claw machine button was being pressed repeatedly.

"Fink! What the fuck is that—" My inquiry was interrupted by a wave of blood that smacked against my mouth, some of which I inadvertently swallowed.

"Never seen it before! Time to swim faster, I guess!" he yelled letting off a cackle at the end.

Janie wasn't asking questions; she was hauling ass. But I noticed she took a precious second here and there to glance back, making sure I was okay.

Suddenly, a monstrous tongue slithered out from the jowl of the titan. It was long and a splotchy shade of salmon. It looked like a diseased rat's tail.

When it dropped into the water, it didn't take long to reach us. Before anyone could react, the three of us had been scooped up in the twirling slimy mucous membrane.

As the powerful muscle retracted, I thought for sure we were about to be devoured. But like many events of late, I found myself surprised.

The enormous, claw-like triple digits extracted us from the tender taste ship and cradled us gently. Then something even more unexpected happened as the giant creature pulled us into its chest.

The three of us sat mushed together. The screaming finally stopped, but the confusion had just begun.

The colossal creature let out a gentle howl. Although it seemed unfathomable, in my mind I almost felt like it was purring with comfort.

"Is it—is it… hugging us?!" I bellowed.

"It certainly seems that way!" Fink laughed.

The mammoth being then dropped us gently onto the soft shores of the island, and in a matter of moments disappeared back into the liquid.

"Well, that was weird," Janie said.

"A lot of weird things happen when you're dead," Fink replied, hopping back to his feet like the experience wasn't too much for him.

We were all stained in red as we approached the towering doorway. It looked like two lips that were sealed tight vertically. Fink did not approach them though. Instead, he stepped toward a rounded nose that was attached to the side of the structure.

There was a plethora of nasal hairs that trickled out of the pair of nostrils. He extended his arm and used his fingers to tickle the hairs ever so slightly.

I stared at the numerous speckling of blackheads that riddled the exterior of the nose, waiting for something to happen. When it started to shake, I didn't know what to expect. That was probably true about most anything that happened since I'd died.

The nose shook until it looked on the verge of explosion. A jarring sneeze erupted that was so earsplitting it nearly knocked me off my feet. I assumed the snout acted as a doorbell, because after the sneeze, the vertical lips parted the gigantic doors, making way for us.

When we made our way inside, I could see Belthorn right away. He was looking out an opening and into the murky waters. It wasn't hard to spot his grainy dark texture and the gamut of spikes that climbed off his surface. He certainly popped out from the pink fleshy background.

I was caught off guard when he turned around and greeted us. The other Thorn we'd encountered upon reentry was so nefarious and distant. I suppose the Thorns are just like people; each of them is unique.

"Hello! Welcome!" Belthorn exclaimed. The nerdy tone

and general friendliness attached to his aura made me feel at ease. I could tell it did the same for Janie.

"Belthorn," Fink said with a nod.

Fink didn't seem incredibly happy to see him. Part of me wondered why, but I hadn't the faintest clue.

"What did you think of Gragrine?" Belthorn was mouthless like the rest of them, but his tender voice being transmitted into my skull didn't really bother me. He seemed really inviting.

"That fucking thing in the blood?" Fink asked.

"Yes."

"Who cares," Fink replied.

"Oh…" Belthorn seemed saddened by the response.

"Well, I've gotta be honest, I was really terrified at first, but it was actually kinda sweet. What is it exactly?" Janie asked.

"I thought you might recognize it. It's a mixture of anteater and gorilla. You see, my people tend to look down on the animal kingdom. They don't find it *entertaining* enough. But I just love animals, so I'm trying to do more with them in this space."

"That's one hell of a start. That thing was cool," I interjected.

"Why, thank you," Belthorn replied. His tone oozed with satisfaction after hearing the compliment.

"Most Thorns aren't willing to dabble. It's all just cutting and fucking to the majority. But I'm a tad different. I enjoy a healthy variety. But my unconventional pleasures have gotten me into trouble in the past."

"Like what?" I asked.

"Happiness for example. That's probably what's gotten me into the most trouble. I actually like quite a few taboo feelings, but things such as compassion and empathy aren't exactly welcomed by my kind. To me they're not just some sort of novelty item, they're exciting! I genuinely feel electrified by them! For whatever reason that makes *me* the weird one though," Belthorn explained.

"Well, what's the old saying? Variety's the spice of life?" I said.

"What a wonderful saying!" Belthorn exclaimed.

"Okay, but we're here on business. Can we get to it? I'm sorry, but I find this whole… conversation incredibly unentertaining," Fink whined.

"You would," Belthorn scoffed. "Regardless, I refuse to stoop to your level, Fink. So, let me then ask, what can I do for you all?"

Fink looked over toward Janie as if prompting her to explain herself.

"Well, Mr. Belthorn, I was murdered recently… by a cold-blooded psychopath. It was really out of left field. I don't think anyone expects to die, but I guess you never know when your number is gonna get called," Janie explained.

"Oh, dear. How dreadful. I'm terribly sorry to hear that," Belthorn replied. He was so kind to her, kinder than most *people* would have even been.

"Thank you. Furthermore, the man I chose to be with while I was alive… he's not a good man. He's not capable of keeping my children safe. In fact, he's a definite danger to them. Fink explained to us that you might be able to help me check on them. Or maybe even get us back to them…"

She said 'us.' We were officially a thing now. I mean, I kind of figured that much, but it was nice to hear out loud.

When Belthorn looked into her eyes he could see the hurt and anguish.

"Come here my child," he said, opening his arms.

As she walked into the prickly ridged exterior to oblige his caring offer, she cried out when the pricks entered her tender skin.

"Apologies," Belthorn said, backing away with a hint of sadness on his face. "This fucking shell I've been confined to… as much as I want to, it's just not designed to allow me to console. Please, I don't think I got your names," he said.

"It's Janie and Andy," Fink replied while rolling his eyes

at the affectionate moment.

"Please, Andy, give her a hug for me," Belthorn said with what sounded like a sniffle.

I did as Belthorn told me and consoled Janie, and wiped the small droplets of blood away from the tiny holes he'd punched into her.

"This just breaks my black heart," he whispered to himself. "Unfortunately, there is no way for me to return you. Being ostracized has left me with little to no authority. I can't show you them, but… I can allow you a glimpse. However, understanding your current position, are you sure that's what you want?"

"Yes."

There wasn't a shred of hesitation in her voice.

"What if you see something terrible? Something you can't stop from happening?" Belthorn asked.

"That's a risk I'm willing to take," Janie replied.

"An eternity full of frustration sounds like a dreadful sentence, so I want to ask you again. Are you sure you want to know?"

"Yes."

"So be it then."

Belthorn raised his prickly arms above his head, and similar to the projection of memories that were suctioned from us upon reentry, a snowy screen manifested above him. But what was on the screen was what he'd feared; it was the last thing Janie would've wanted to see.

Bell and Alicia's room was filled with darkness. They were both so young and innocent. It was obvious they were missing something. They were missing their mother.

Alicia grabbed onto two of the bars surrounding her cradle. She couldn't have been more than a couple of years old. The fright manipulating her expression was an emotion that shouldn't have graced her at such an age, if ever.

Across the room from her, baby Bell laid on her back. The shrill screeches she emitted carved into Janie's soul as she watched on. She couldn't seem to stop the tears and sadness. The child needed someone to be there with her, but her mother had moved on.

Suddenly, the darkness began to stir and move. From out of the shadows Paul emerged, an oversized Budweiser can in his hand. He staggered into the room, only adding to the noise.

"Shut the fuck up!" he screamed, while throwing back another massive gulp of the cheap beer. "You're going to be fucking quiet, one way, or another!"

Paul dropped the beer can and the little contents that remained fizzed onto the floor. He put both of his hands on his belt buckle and undid it. Then he unbuttoned his jeans and unzipped his fly, aiming his manhood at his hysterical child.

As the urine rushed from the head of his cock, baby Bell's moans of anguish were cut short. The bubbling choke of hot piss obstructing her airway replaced the cries.

As the urine drenched her newborn skin, Janie cried out, "You fucking bastard! I'll kill you!"

Belthorn cut the projection, knowing it was a bad idea, but feeling it was his place to make the decision for Janie.

"I'm so sorry, my dear," he whispered solemnly. I could tell he felt guilt in showing her, but I knew he was only trying to help.

Janie fell to the ground crying. Even though there were no tears it was a heart-wrenching sight to see. I slumped down on the floor beside her and wrapped both arms around her. I held her tight and stared at my own forearm mindlessly. I didn't know what else I could possibly do. There was no way for me to change what she'd seen.

Then suddenly, I was struck with a jolt that felt electrical. My body shook about violently and I fell backward.

I couldn't speak.

I couldn't move.

I couldn't feel.

"Andy?!" Janie yelled in shock. "Baby, what's wrong?"

Another powerful shock crashed into my body, causing

me to start trembling all over. Janie reached for my hand but I couldn't sense her touch. It was a horrible realization.

"What's happening to him?!" she yelled, looking back at Belthorn and Fink.

The pudgy man that had helped me on the most recent stretch of my odyssey stood wide-eyed as the words left his lips: "They're bringing him back."

THE RETURN

Coming back was a lot different than my descent. There was nothing scary about it in comparison to all I'd witnessed. Just some bright light, the typical special effects according to Fink. The most sickening part was being torn away from Janie. Even though we had found each other in the most unconventional and alien environment, as I was being ripped away, I didn't care.

I missed eternity and I missed Janie. In a lot of ways there was far less to worry about in the space that we explored and fell in love within. As soon as I opened my eyes, my heart taking to its rhythm again, it was back to all the problems.

The coma had lasted a little over two weeks. The medical technicians told me it was a miracle I'd even survived the shooting.

They explained that, initially, I had been pronounced clinically dead, and for hours my situation looked hopeless. The amount of time I'd spent with Janie felt like an eternity, but was it only a few hours? I couldn't be sure how time correlated between 'real life' and the afterlife.

I spent a few more months in the hospital because I had no one in my life to look after me. That didn't bother me though. I preferred the isolation. I had quite a bit to think about. My tale wasn't exactly the kind of story you could just tell someone over a morning coffee. They'd think you were batshit crazy. I'd have never believed it myself had someone tried to sell me on it.

I wished Janie could have somehow been there with me, but she was dead, and as far as Belthorn knew, there was no loophole. Phillip was dead too, that piece of shit, as well as Tatiana. There were moments I wondered what became of her. Was there a way to get stuck upon reentry? She never made it past the horrible worms. I wondered if I would have suffered the same fate had I slipped off that narrow bridge. I should've asked Fink while I had the chance.

Was any of that real? Was it all some nightmare within my period of limbo? Or am I completely fucking insane? I wondered, as I listened to the annoying beep of medical machinery beside me.

No.

I didn't believe so.

There was no way that all of it could just be some strange hallucination. Everything lined up too perfectly for that to be the case. Everyone that was there with me was dead, and JC survived with minor injuries. Injuries, might I add, that were eerily similar to those that I'd witnessed when the Thorn had played back Phillip's macabre memory for his enjoyment.

Still, once I was finally well enough to return home, I found myself tossing and turning in bed. I couldn't eat, I couldn't sleep, I couldn't cry. I was numb. Janie couldn't do any of those things either. I wondered where she was. I wondered if she was watching me at that very moment.

"Janie, I love you!" I shouted, hoping that she was peeping in on me in a voyeuristic fashion.

I heard a trio of thunderous slams on the wall of my apartment. *Is it Janie?*

"Keep it the fuck down in there! It's 3 AM!"

No, it wasn't Janie. Janie wouldn't be such a fucking cunt.

My mind continued to race for days and days. I poured over all the details, wrote out every idea and memory in the moleskin journal by my bedside. But, no matter how many times I dissected it and put it back together, I always came to the same conclusion: I didn't want to be alive.

It was pretty simple. I knew that if I died, I was going right back to the same place. I would be reunited with Janie. I knew the area well enough to find Fink again, and I assumed he would be able to locate her, or at least have some idea of her whereabouts.

Even if I walked mindlessly for eternity, sifting through aisle after aisle of violence and depravity, it would be better than living a lie. Better than just being some lowbrow entertainment for a savage species (Belthorn aside; he was cool as shit). The bottom line was I wasn't going to be happy until I was dead again.

Not only did I have no purpose before, but on top of that, I now knew with total certainty that *there was* no purpose. And all of those people that filled up churches, and those that subscribed to positivity, were all bowing to a massive illusion. They were in for a rude fucking awakening.

Within a few weeks I settled on it. I had it all figured out. Everything except for one question. The impossible aspect was that the question wasn't for me; it was for Janie.

If I had the chance to bring them back with me, is that what you'd want? I pondered.

But as far as I knew, there was no way to ask a dead girl a question. I would just have to decide for myself.

A BITTERSWEET BEGINNING

I couldn't fuck it up. If I got locked up in prison that would truly be torture, worse than any that could be inflicted upon me if I returned to eternity. I didn't imagine it would be too difficult; it wasn't as if I was actually trying to get away with anything.

There was still one final test before I could be sure that things were what they seemed. Before I could be sure that the life-altering impressions that were imprinted upon my psyche so realistically were in fact that of reality. But I wouldn't know until I was inside the house.

I exited the car and unlocked the trunk. I looked down at the shotgun and the large box of shells. It was easy enough to acquire; after a waiting period of just a few days I was ready to rock n' roll. I'd shot it off in the woods near some hunting land the prior evening. It worked like a charm.

I should only need a few of the shells, but I loaded it up to the five-cartridge maximum. You never can be too prepared, and this was one event I didn't want to come up short on. The barrel of the gun was long, so I purchased a trench coat for a reasonable price elsewhere.

I tossed a few more shells in my pocket for good measure and hid the weapon on the interior of my coat. As I approached the house, I carefully checked each of the windows, examining both the first and second floors. All the lights were off, as they should be in the dead of night.

I made my way around the back of the house to the patio. I wanted to avoid creating any noise if I could. A nice suburban area such as this, with a drunk piece of shit watching over it, was bound to have an unlocked door or window around the perimeter.

When I turned that first handle and didn't feel resistance, my heart *really* started to pound. It felt like it was going to crawl up my throat as I stepped into the black confines of the patio. The door that led into the kitchen was wide open, so I cautiously tiptoed forward.

There was a large pile of unopened mail sitting on the table. I hadn't quite envisioned it would be this easy, but there it was… the final test.

I reached over with my free hand and sifted through the stack quietly until I found it. I didn't pay any attention to the envelope aside from where the name was printed. In black inky letters it read: Paul Watson.

That solidified it for me. Even if somehow, I'd had an intense dream in my coma that just happened to include the correct murdered teammates at Bank USA, there was no way to explain how I knew Janie's piece of shit husband's name. I didn't know dick about her, aside for the occasional daydream that I concocted in my own skull.

As I crept up the steps, I readied my gun. When I entered the first room on the left, I received further validation. It was decorated exactly as I remembered seeing it in Belthorn's conjured depiction.

The same cribs sat across from each other.

The same cartoonish wallpaper covered the background.

The same dimensions outlined the area.

It was the same room, there was no doubt about it.

The babies slept good for once. They didn't seem to be fearful or in any discomfort. I planned to suffocate them with a pillow; it seemed like the simplest and most painless way to go about it. It should be quiet, and I could also avoid altering their appearance. This way if Janie observed their funerals, they would look just as she remembered them.

I leaned the shotgun against the crib carefully and lifted the extra pillow from the feet of baby Bell.

"Don't worry, Daddy won't piss on your face again, sweetheart," I whispered.

As I pressed the pillow down against her face, no noise could be heard. The cloth snuffed it out entirely, which made things easy enough. As her little limbs flailed about, I felt evil. Even though I knew the means to the end, it didn't make me feel any better inside. I prayed, forgetting it didn't matter for a moment, that Janie didn't happen to be checking in on the kids that particular evening. Or me, for that matter.

Suddenly, baby Bell's limbs came to a standstill; all life had left her tiny frame. Without warning a loud scream invaded the room, followed by some childish crying. Little Alicia had awoken. She was probably frightened by the dark man in her room looming over her dead sister's crib. That was not part of the plan.

As the lights quickly came on, I snatched up the shotgun simultaneously. What I faced next there was simply no way to account for.

"Who—Who are you?! What do you want?" I had no clue who the fifty-something-year-old woman standing in the doorway was. I held the gun steady on her nonetheless.

"I'm sorry? Who are *you*?" I asked.

"We don't want any trouble."

"I'm not going to hurt you, just tell me your name."

"Susan, it's Susan Tines! I'm—I'm their grandmother," she explained as her hands started to shake and tears welled up in her eyes.

"Tines… shit," I mumbled. It hit me like a load of bricks; the last name was different. Janie's mom must've stayed over to help out.

"Hi, Susan… I don't have much time, I've gotta be quick. This is gonna sound absolutely fucking Looney Tunes, but I promise you it's the truth. A few months ago, I died alongside your daughter. I died trying to save her life. We met in the afterlife and… we fell in love. She misses her babies; she would want me to bring them back to her," I explained.

Susan finally moved her eyes off the gun and into the crib, where Bell's body remained completely limp. Then, all of the sudden, Alicia wasn't the only one screaming.

"Get down in the corner and shut the fuck up, please," I commanded, taking one hand off the gun to retrieve the pillow.

I took a few sidesteps toward Alicia's crib and used my free arm to muscle her down. It wasn't difficult to get her face full of the cloth. My hand was big enough that my fingers wrapped around each side of her head, keeping it steady in place and obstructing her airways.

The jerking limbs began to lose most of their steam. Susan continued to watch me suffocate her granddaughter in absolute shock. Her cries were muffled but still audible.

"Shhhhh," I whispered. "We're almost done, it's almost over now."

Then, out of the blue, a new voice entered the equation. "God damn it! Susan! Can you shut that fucking kid up! Please! I'm trying to sleep this off! I thought that's what you were here for!" Paul yelled.

I could hear him getting out of bed and, oh boy, was he in for a fucking surprise. When the sick bastard entered the room, his expression was one of infuriation. But that was quickly exchanged for fear and horror.

When he got to looking through the doorway, Susan was still squatting petrified in the corner, and I sat slumped on the ground facing him. Dead baby Bell's tiny unresponsive body was laid out to my left, and Alicia's static corpse was to my right.

I knew he wanted to just run away and leave Susan to fend for herself, but I pulled the trigger before he had a chance. The hot steel erupted and sprayed his calf. The shot was accurate enough to blow most of it clean off him.

The freshly ravaged area of unmade flesh collapsed in on itself. As he fell to the ground screaming and in shock, I asked him with hyper excitement, "You done shaking and pissing on fucking babies, pal?!"

His pathetic cries continued as the river of red flowed like a human dam had broken. The light glistened off the exposed bone shard that exited his mangled leg. The look on his face was priceless.

"Paul," I called out.

I waited for him to stop screaming and refocus. That moment hadn't come yet, and I was growing impatient. In his shell-shocked state he couldn't offer me the slightest acknowledgement.

"Asshole! I'm talking to you! Answer me or the next one goes between your fucking eyes!"

I was bluffing him, of course. The last thing I wanted was to be thrust into some odyssey with that piece of shit. Talk about awkward.

"I'm—I'm fucking dying, man," he mumbled.

"You deserve death, or at least I used to think someone like you would… but that's not the case. You'll live, trust me on that. But first tell me you're done hurting children. Say it and we can all move on!"

"I'm—I'm all done," he mustered through the rainfall of teardrops.

"Never again?"

"Never again, I swear!" he cried.

"Thank you," I said, pulling out my cellphone.

Susan was still screaming, but did so in a low tone, remaining in place. I was glad she was being obedient; I didn't want this thing to go sideways.

I dialed 911 and seconds later an operator was on the line with me.

"Hello? Yeah, I need an ambulance to… what's the address here?" I directed the query at Susan because Paul seemed too overwhelmed at the moment.

"11 Park Ave, West Strasburg," Susan spoke like she'd seen a ghost, probably because she had.

I relayed the address back to the operator and told them there was a gunshot wound and a lot of blood. Hopefully, they would be there quickly.

"Okay," I said getting ready to put the gun in my mouth. But before I could, something struck me. *I wonder if Janie would want me to bring her mom with me too? The least I can do is ask Susan,* I thought.

"Susan, if I told you that I could let you see your daughter and both your granddaughters, all together at once, right now, what would you say? The only downside is that you'd have to leave everything and everyone else behind."

The repulsion and shockwaves pulsating over her face were profound. Her jaw rattled relentlessly but nothing seemed to come out.

"Would you like me to choose for you?" I asked.

"I—I—I'd like to wait if that's alright by you," she begged after releasing the stutter of the century.

"Fair enough," I replied with a smile.

Then I stuck the hot barrel of the gun into my mouth and pulled on the trigger.

REENTRY

I was hoping there wouldn't be so much torture in the beginning this time, but I was wrong. It was pretty close to the same thing. It was the same black tunnel. It was the same crimson lava pool. The same big red eyes in the sky, and the same multi-limbed abominations ripping me apart as easy as pulled pork. I couldn't believe that torture could feel so cookie-cutter and prepackaged, but to my chagrin it did. In the beginning anyway.

Part of me had hoped that they'd recognize me. That they'd know that I'd been through it all before and understand that I didn't need any further hardening. It was only a few months ago, I hadn't forgotten yet. Too bad they didn't have a punch card for frequent customers.

When the parasites invaded my body, I fantasized about reconnecting with Janie. Would she be happy with my decision? I wouldn't have done it if I didn't believe so in my heart. Would she want her children living an emotional façade with an alcoholic serial abuser? No way.

As my naked body bolted down the dark tunnel I was once again nearing the end. My squirmy friends would steer me in the direction of the hole to live out morbid fantasies and try and fuck with my head. I was ready for it, but I just hoped I would be reconnected with Bell and Alicia on the other side of the flesh.

***

The initial murder simulation felt faster. It was probably because it wasn't my first rodeo. I knew what the deal was, I knew the fix was in, and how it ended. So, as I was shit out through the rubbery hole, I actually felt pretty prepared.

I landed in the middle of league night at a busy bowling alley. My surroundings made me feel semi-comfortable, so I wasn't too concerned. Sure, the fellas at the alley looked nice enough, but as I was cracking open their faces and heads with a 16-pound ball, I didn't feel a whole lot.

I didn't feel bad.

I didn't feel good.

I didn't feel anything.

The entire process seemed boring. They weren't real; they couldn't be. And even if they were, what exactly was death anyway to me now?

Certainly not what it was before. As I forced an old man's head into the unforgiving rapid-spin belt of the ball return, I accepted it was merely a vehicle. The rubbery skin that was torn from his wrinkly face, the blood that splattered everywhere and all over my naked body, it was all just entertainment. It wasn't that serious.

***

When I entered the second part of my perverse preparation, I was dropped into the back of a burger joint on a busy day. Again, I can't say I felt too much.

The staff at Burger Billy's were mostly impoverished